"TOO SMART" JONES

and the Stolen Bicycles

D0096175

7

A GILBERT
MORRIS
MYSTERY

"TOO SMART" JONES and the Stolen Bicycles

MOODY PRESS
CHICAGO

ISBN: 0-8024-4031-2

1 3 5 7 9 10 8 6 4 2

Printed in the United States of America

Contents

1

Juliet's At It Again

It must be nice to have a sister that's so smart." Chili Williams was sitting on a playground bench beside one of his best friends, Joe Jones. They watched as several other boys shot baskets on the court.

Joe scowled at him. "That's what you think! How would you like to live with somebody who always makes better grades than you do? I'm ten, and she's just a year older, and she's always doing better than I am."

Chili grinned. He was wearing a bright green shirt today and a cap that was turned backward on his head. "Why don't you just let her do all the homework—the stuff you don't want to do—and you could do the fun stuff like inventing?" He knew how much Joe Jones loved to invent things.

"It doesn't work that way," Joe complained.

"I thought when we started being home-schooled it would be easy, but Mom and Dad are tougher than any schoolteachers I ever had. We have to do our own homework. They let Juliet help me a little but not much."

Just then a boy in a wheelchair shot across the court in their direction. "Hey, what's coming down here?" he yelled. Suddenly he reversed the wheels and spun the wheelchair so fast it made Chili blink. Then he braked in front of them, grinning. "How was that?"

Chili grinned back at his friend. "That was great, Flash. You're gonna break your neck someday, though." He knew that Melvin Gordon, always known as Flash, never felt sorry for himself in spite of being in a wheelchair. Of the Oakwood Support Group for homeschoolers, he was probably the happiest and most outgoing. Flash always insisted that someday he would get out of his wheelchair and walk. God would do it.

Joe kept on complaining about having to do math. But Flash was studying Chili's face. He said, "What's the matter, Chili? You got troubles today?"

"Oh, it's nothing."

"Sure it's something," Flash insisted. "I can tell."

"What are you? A mind reader?"

"No, but I can tell when a friend is feeling down."

"That's right," Joe said. "You haven't talked much today. Don't you feel good?"

Chili shrugged his shoulders. He picked up his basketball and began tossing it back and forth from one hand to the other. "Well, I do feel pretty sad," he said. "My bike's missing."

Just then Billy Rollins joined them. He was big for his ten years. He pulled a Snickers from his pocket, stripped away the paper, and chomped off a bite. Talking around the huge mouthful, he said, "Who would steal that old wreck of a bike you've got?"

Chili Williams did not usually have a hot temper, but somehow this remark from Billy Rollins irritated him.

"Nobody would want that old thing! One of your friends just took it to bug you," Billy went on.

"No friend of mine would do a thing like that—except you, Billy."

Billy Rollins just grinned and took another bite. "That old thing"—you could hardly understand what he was saying—"if I did steal it, I'd haul it right out to the dump. I wouldn't want a thing like that messing up my yard."

Suddenly Chili found himself doing something that he had never done before. He got up from the bench and pushed Billy with both hands. Hard. "You just stop it!" he said. "That was a good bike!"

Billy Rollins immediately threw himself

back at Chili and shoved. In seconds, the two boys were in a scuffling match, grabbing at each other and trying to knock one another down.

Flash yelled at them from his wheelchair. "Now you guys cut that out!"

"Yeah," Joe said, and he stepped between them. Just as he did, Billy Rollins's shoulder caught him, and he went down sprawling onto the concrete. Up he jumped. "Who do you think you're shoving, Billy Rollins?"

Too Smart Jones and several friends were swinging each other on the park playground swings. Juliet was just at the top of her swing when she saw a fight begin across the basketball court. As soon as she could slow down the swing, she jumped off, yelling, "Come on! The boys are getting into a fight!" She started to run, auburn ponytail flapping.

"Come on," she yelled again. Juliet knew her two best friends, Jenny White and Delores Del Rio, were right at her heels.

The three girls ran up to the battling boys, and Juliet jumped right into the middle of things. First, she grabbed a handful of Billy Rollins's hair and jerked him back. "You leave my brother alone, Billy!"

"Ow!" Billy yelled and pushed Juliet so hard that she lost her balance and sat down.

"That's it!" Joe said. "I'm going to bust you one!"

10

"No!" Juliet cried, scrambling to her feet. "Stop that fighting!"

Flash suddenly wheeled his chair between Billy and the other boys. "We don't need to fight. That's no way to act, you guys."

Chili appeared to be sort of ashamed of himself. He said, "Yeah, we don't need to fight."

"Well, seeing that you're apologizing, I'll let you off this time," Billy said, dusting himself off. He took out another candy bar.

"You shouldn't have said what you did about my bike, though, Billy," Chili insisted. "That's one of the best bikes ever made. It's a Schwinn."

"Why are you arguing over your *bike?*" Juliet asked, pushing her hair back into order.

"I was just telling the guys that someone stole my bike."

"Oh, that's awful!" Jenny White cried. She was always very sympathetic. "Maybe someone just borrowed it, Chili."

"Nope. I wish that was true, but it's not. It's just gone."

"That's too bad," Delores said. She was a small, well-built girl. Her parents had been circus acrobats, and both Delores and her brother had inherited their talent. "I just remembered something. There's a boy in our neighborhood —I don't know if you know him—Willard Powell. He told me just yesterday that someone had stolen *his* bike."

At that moment Too Smart Jones put her hands behind her back and became very still. She frowned. Her mind was working hard. *Two bikes are missing,* she was thinking. *From different neighborhoods, but the neighborhoods aren't far apart.*

Joe saw her frown. "Uh-oh!" he said. "Juliet's at it again."

"Watch out!" Flash cried. "Too Smart Jones is about to swing into action!"

Everybody laughed, for Juliet had a reputation for wanting to solve mysteries.

"I *wish* you wouldn't call me that! You know how I hate it!"

"I know what you're thinking," Delores said. "Two bikes are gone, all right, but it's probably just a coincidence."

"That's right," Billy Rollins said, and he shrugged. "Some kids don't have any sense. They leave bikes somewhere and forget where they put them."

"I *didn't* leave my bike someplace," Chili protested.

Juliet forced herself to smile. "I'm glad you never do anything like that, Billy."

Billy chewed on his new candy bar. "It's good for you other kids to have somebody to look up to."

A groan went up at this, and Joe muttered, "Not a chance."

Juliet just listened as they continued to

talk. Billy kept on tormenting her by calling her Too Smart Jones and making fun of her mystery solving. She ignored him.

She kept thinking, *It's just too much of a coincidence that two bikes would disappear at the same time,* she thought. *This may turn out to be something I'll have to look into.*

2

More Mystery

Juliet and Joe walked along behind their parents. They were going home from their church where the homeschool Support Group had just had an early Friday morning meeting. Juliet was deep in thought about the missing bicycles.

All of a sudden her father turned around and said, "And what's my girl thinking about?" Unexpectedly, he picked up Juliet and tossed her in the air. He was very fit from outdoor work and lots of exercise.

"Daddy, put me down! I'm not a little girl anymore!"

"Oh, I forgot! You're a grown-up young lady." Mr. Jones put down his daughter and looked at her fondly. "You used to like it when I did that."

"I know, but I'm too old for things like that now."

"I beg your pardon!" He grinned and winked at their mother. "We have a grown-up young lady here, Rachel."

Mrs. Jones had auburn hair like Juliet's. She was a very pretty lady, and she was wearing a dress that matched her brown eyes. "She's growing up, all right."

"You've got to do something about Juliet," Joe suddenly piped up. He had on a ball cap. It was turned bill forward, for his parents could not stand anyone's wearing a cap backward or sideways. "She's doing it again, she is."

"Doing what again?" Mr. Jones gave him a questioning look.

"She's trying to solve another mystery. She's *always* trying to solve mysteries. She thinks she's Sherlock Holmes."

"Joe, you be quiet!"

"I won't either be quiet! You can't tell me what to do!"

"Mom and Dad don't want to hear your silly ideas!" Juliet said. She tried to change the subject.

Joe, however, would not shut up. As they walked along, he kept on talking. "She found a new crime to solve. First thing you know, you'll see her picture in the newspaper. 'Girl detective breaks up ring of bicycle thieves.'"

"Bicycle thieves?" Their dad showed interest. "What's that all about?"

"Chili's bicycle was stolen. And Delores told us about Willard Somebody, who lives in their neighborhood. His bike's missing, too, so Juliet thinks a bunch of criminals have moved into town."

"I didn't say anything like that!" Juliet protested.

"You didn't say it, but I saw your eyes!"

"What do you mean you saw my eyes?"

"I mean when you get to thinking, your eyes get crossed."

"They do not!"

"They do too! And you start getting wrinkles in your forehead! Yep, Too Smart Jones is out to solve a mystery again!"

"Now, leave your sister alone, Joe," Mrs. Jones said. "You're always exaggerating."

"I think we'll just let the police take care of solving the crimes around here," their dad said with a smile. He put his arm around Juliet as they walked. "Juliet's just always interested in things, and I think that's good."

"Thanks, Dad," Juliet said gratefully.

It was a beautiful summer day with blue sky overhead and white, fluffy clouds tumbling over one another.

"Look at those birds—what are they doing?" Joe said suddenly.

Everybody glanced at several sparrows beside the curb ahead. A piece of bread was in the gutter, and they were fighting over it, tumbling about and pecking at each other.

Joe laughed. "I thought birds were supposed to get along. Birds are just like people. Look at that one there. He looks like Billy Rollins."

"And you shouldn't always be picking on Billy," Mrs. Jones said.

"Picking on him! He's picking on me!"

"They got into a fight this morning," Juliet said and then immediately regretted saying anything about what had happened.

"What's this about a fight?" Mr. Jones demanded.

And then it all had to come out.

When Joe had finished telling his story, and Mr. Jones had warned him about proper behavior, her brother gave Juliet a harsh look. "I'll get you for that," he muttered.

"I'm sorry, Joe. It just popped out."

"It wasn't a fight anyhow. It was just a shoving match."

Juliet did feel bad about mentioning the fight or argument or whatever it was. She decided to make it up to Joe. "I'll tell you what I'll do. I'll make you some chocolate chip cookies."

"How many?" he asked.

"Two dozen."

"Oh boy, I can pig out on those!"

* * *

After lunch, Juliet went up to her bedroom.

It was a very nice bedroom. The walls were light blue with a border running along the top. The ceiling was painted white, and Juliet had placed glow-in-the-dark stars on it so that when she went to bed she could look at the constellations. The two large windows were covered with frilly white curtains.

She sat at her desk, took out a tablet, and picked up a ballpoint pen. She wrote for some time, putting down all the facts about Chili's bike—the color, the make, the condition it was in. Then she put away the pen and sighed with satisfaction. "You've got to get all the facts if you want to solve crimes," she told herself.

At that moment the phone rang. She did not have her own phone, and her mother picked up the downstairs phone at the same time as she picked up the upstairs one.

"It's me—Jenny."

"Oh, I'll take it, Mom," Juliet said. When she heard her mother hang up, she said, "Hi, Jenny. What's going on?"

"Oh, nothing much. I'm just having some trouble with my grammar lesson. I can't understand what they mean by some of these words. What's the difference between a common noun and a proper noun?"

"Oh, that's easy!" Juliet said. "A common

19

noun is the name of something that's well . . . well, just common . . . like girl or tree or dog or house. Not specific like somebody's name."

"Then what's a proper noun?"

"It's the name of a special person or place—like 'Jenny White' is a proper noun. 'Girl' is a common noun."

"Oh, well, that is easy, isn't it!" Jenny exclaimed. "I don't know why I don't see these things."

"Say, Jenny, I was going to call you anyway. Can you find out if there's been any bikes stolen in your neighborhood?"

"Sure! I'll do that."

Then Juliet called Delores.

"Hi, Delores. This is Juliet."

"Sure. You think I don't know your voice? You don't sound like anybody else."

"I guess not. Well, Delores, can you tell me anything about the bike that was stolen from your neighborhood?"

"I can find out. I'll ask Willard. He just lives a block away."

"Do that, will you?"

"Are you getting all the facts together to solve this case?"

"Oh, it's not really a case yet."

"Sounds like one to me." Delores laughed. "Anyway, I'll check and find out."

Juliet hung up, and for a while she was busy with her schoolwork.

Then Delores called back, and Juliet carefully jotted down all the information about Willard Powell's bike. When she had finished, she compared the facts she had about both missing bicycles.

"There's nothing special about them. They're just both boys' bikes." She sighed and put the tablet away, being careful to put it in her drawer under some papers. She didn't leave things like that lying around. If Joe found it, he would make fun of her.

Then Juliet lay down on the bed, put on her headphones, and listened to music for a while. Her black-and-white cat, Boots, jumped up on the bed and then onto her stomach.

Juliet liked being alone like this. She liked being with her friends and family too, but sometimes she wanted to be in her room with the door shut, listening to music, or reading, or just thinking. She thought, *I'm lucky to have a room like this all by myself. Not every girl in the world has it this nice. The Lord has been especially good to me.*

She had almost dozed off when the telephone rang again, so she did not pick it up.

And then her door burst open.

Juliet sat up. "Don't bother to knock, Joe! Just come charging in!"

"Guess what's happened!"

"I don't know what's happened. What?"

"Sam Del Rio just called. You know what he told me?"

"Of course I don't know what he told you."

"He told me—" Joe looked out the window. He had an odd expression on his face. "He told me that his bike is missing."

Juliet came off the bed, ripping away the headphones. "What did you say?"

"Sam's bike is missing. I'm going over to talk to him. You want to come?"

"Sure, I want to come!" Juliet retrieved her tablet from the drawer and stuck the pen in her pocket. She saw the cat staring at her with big green eyes. "You can't go this time, Boots."

Boots said, *"Mrow!"* Then he put down his head and closed his eyes.

"That cat's gotten plumb lazy," Joe said. "Come on. Let's race."

They ran to the garage and unchained their bikes. Then they whizzed down the street.

Joe was younger, but he was stronger and could beat Juliet every time. "You may be Too Smart," he yelled back, "but you're not as good a bicycle rider as I am!"

3

The Clue

On the way to the Del Rio house, Juliet had a sudden thought. She called ahead to Joe, "Joe—Joe! Let's go by and see if Jenny wants to go with us!"

"OK."

Joe cut his bike around, let Juliet go by, then sailed past her again. "I'm riding circles around you!" he yelled with delight. "Catch me if you can."

Juliet pumped as hard as she could, but she could never quite manage to catch Joe. *I'm going to practice,* she thought. *I'm going to beat him one of these days!*

By the time they reached Jenny's house, Juliet was panting. She put the kickstand in place and ran up to the front door.

Jenny's mother came at her knock, and Juliet said, "Hello, Mrs. White."

"Not Mrs. White anymore."

"Oh, that's right. You're Mrs. Tanner now. Hey, I'm sorry."

"That's all right. It takes awhile to get used to new names."

At that moment Jenny popped up beside her mother. "Hi, Juliet. What's going on?"

"Joe and I are going over to the Del Rios and thought you might like to come along."

"Can I, Mom?"

"Of course. You go on and have a good time." Mrs. Tanner smiled knowingly. "And I know what you'll do. You'll go up into that attic and try on clothes."

Jenny laughed. "We probably will."

"We like to do that," Juliet said. "And besides that, Mrs. Del Rio can cook like crazy. I love her Mexican food."

"Well, be careful on those bicycles."

"We will, Mom."

The two girls rolled their bikes to the street, where Joe waited.

He said, "The two of you together ought to be able to ride twice as fast as I can. Let's see you do it."

Jenny grinned. "That's like a cowboy saying he carries two guns because one doesn't shoot far enough."

"Hey, that's a good one, Jenny! OK, let's go."

The trio pedaled down the street with Joe teasing the girls about how slow they were.

24

As they rode, Jenny said, "Juliet—I should tell you—there's a boy who lives down the street from me. Jerry Stone. His bicycle is missing."

"*What!*" Juliet frowned. Then she remembered what Joe had said about her eyes crossing when she was thinking. It was nonsense, of course, but she blinked anyway and looked straight ahead. "We've got to get to the bottom of this," she said.

The Del Rio house was different from most. It had a big brick wall around it. The house was set way back, and there were flowers and trees everywhere. It was very old and had a huge attic, which the girls loved because it had trunks full of old clothes. There was a mirror up there, too, so they could see themselves as they played dress up.

"Let's see what Sam can tell us about his bike," Juliet said.

Grandfather Del Rio met them at the door as they walked up the front steps. He was a fine looking man with silvery hair. He had been in the circus himself when he was young.

"Ah, we have company, I see! Come in, my young friends."

"We came over to see Sam and Delores," Juliet said with a smile. She liked Mr. Del Rio very much. He was friendly, and he could tell wonderful stories about his early days in the circus.

"I will get them for you. But in the meanwhile, why don't you come into the kitchen, and we will see what there is to eat."

"That sounds good to me!" Joe said at once. He sniffed the air hungrily. "Mrs. Del Rio can cook like nothing I ever saw."

"Ah, I always said that was why I married her." Mr. Del Rio grinned broadly. "But that was not the only reason. She also was the most beautiful girl I ever saw." At that moment his wife entered from the kitchen door. "And she is still the most beautiful woman I ever saw."

Mrs. Del Rio too had silvery hair. She pretended to be cross, and she said, "If you think you're going to get out of cutting the grass by flattering me, you're mistaken!"

"Ah, my dear wife, how can you think such a thing?" Mr. Del Rio put his arm around her shoulders and gave her a hug. "We have been married so many years, and I have enjoyed every second of it."

"I can think of a few times you didn't seem to be enjoying it."

"Ah, but I was. You must know that."

At that moment Sam and Delores burst in and greeted their visitors.

Then the five youngsters headed for the back patio. On the way, they passed through the kitchen, where they picked up two cookies each. Mrs. Del Rio said, "You can't have more, because we're going to have something really good later on."

"Boy, it's nice to have cookies on demand. Your grandmother must bake every day."

"She does, Joe," Delores said. "She loves to cook."

"She makes world-class cookies." When he had finished both of his, he noticed that Juliet had eaten only one of hers. "I'll eat that one, Juliet."

"You will not!"

"I'd better eat it. It's going to make you fat." He reached out to take it, and Juliet slapped away his hand.

"Keep your hands off my cooky, Joe Jones!"

"You two can fight at home!" Sam told them cheerfully. He was eleven, the same age as Juliet, and had black hair and dark eyes. "What are you guys up to?"

"We came over to find out about your bike."

Sam's face fell. "Yeah, that was a good bike," he said. "Who would steal a kid's bike? That's what I want to know."

"We just heard somebody stole Jerry Stone's bike, too," Delores said. "It was a nice tenspeed. He got it for his birthday last year. He was about ready to cry over it."

"I don't blame him," Joe said. "I'd feel like crying if somebody stole my bicycle."

"Yeah, and what's even worse," Sam said,

"Jerry's parents have grounded him because he didn't take care of it."

"That's tough. To lose your bike and get grounded too."

"Well, let's look around your yard and see if we can find any clues," Juliet said.

"We've already looked," Sam said. "Couldn't find a thing."

Delores pulled Juliet's ponytail. "But we're not good detectives like Juliet is."

"So get to work, Too Smart," Joe told her.

Juliet sniffed. She had long ago given up on persuading Joe to stop calling her Too Smart. She turned to Samuel. "When was the last time you saw your bike, and did you see anything different about where it was?"

Juliet listened as Sam told her the circumstances of the missing bicycle.

"We didn't see anything different," Delores said. "They just came and got it and left. Whoever 'they' were."

"Still, maybe there's something. They weren't ghosts. They had to walk in on their own feet. What about footprints?"

"Nothing showed. The ground was dry. Besides, the bike was parked on the patio, and that's concrete. They must be pretty nervy," Sam said gloomily, "to come right onto somebody's patio."

Juliet looked and looked, and so did everybody else, but they failed to find anything un-usual.

"I'm really mad about this," Sam said, looking crosser than ever. "That's the first new bike I ever had."

"Before," Delores said, "Sam just had an old one that Grandfather painted to make it look good."

"But this one was brand-new."

"I know that it had some odd name I'd never heard of, and I can't remember it," Juliet said.

"It's a Raleigh, and it was made in England. It was a *really* good bike."

"Well, I told you over and over again, and so did Grandfather, to lock your bike up to something or put it in the garage," Delores told him.

"I know. I should have done that," Sam said. "But I just didn't. Wow, a fellow makes a mistake one time, and then he loses his bike because of it."

They were still looking around the yard when Juliet found a candy wrapper out by the sidewalk. She held up the small paper, read what was on it, and said, "Here's a candy bar wrapper for your trash."

"What is it—a Snickers?" Sam asked, coming her way. "If it is, it's mine. I'll take it."

"No, it's got a name I never heard of."

"Let me see it," Joe said. "I'm an expert on candy bars." He took the wrapper and squinted

29

at it. "Fudgy. I never heard of a Fudgy bar before."

"Neither have I," Delores said.

"Fudgy. Well, this may be a clue."

"A candy wrapper? Out here by the street?" Sam shook his head. "No way. People go by here all the time. If you'd found it in the yard, I would have said yes."

Juliet said, "You're probably right." Nevertheless she put the Fudgy wrapper in her pocket. She would think more about it later.

"Come in now! We'll have a little something to eat!" Mrs. Del Rio called from the kitchen door.

The group ran for the house, and soon they were sitting about the round kitchen table eating tacos.

"You sure know how to make tacos, Mrs. Del Rio," Joe said. He took a huge bite. "They're even better than last time."

"We'd better not eat too much, or Mom will say we've spoiled our supper," Juliet warned him.

"Here. Try some of this on it, Joe."

Joe took the small bottle that Mr. Del Rio handed him. "What is it?"

"Just a little hot sauce."

"You better be careful with that," Sam advised. "It'll take the top of your head off."

Joe Jones could never refuse a challenge. He put four or five drops on his taco.

30

"That's too much!" Delores cried.

"Don't worry. I can handle it."

Joe took a huge bite and two or three healthy chews. Suddenly his face turned red, and his eyes flew open wide. "Help!" he cried. He leaped to his feet and began to run around the kitchen.

"What's the matter?" Juliet screamed. She jumped up, but when she tried to stop him, he would only shake his head and point at his mouth.

"Here," Sam yelled. He picked up a glass of water and handed it to Joe, who immediately began drinking. Some of the water spilled down his pullover front.

Juliet said, "Is he going to be all right?"

"Yes, yes. He just got too much hot sauce," Mr. Del Rio said.

"I tried to warn him. That stuff is like liquid fire." Sam grinned knowingly.

Finally Joe was able to whisper, "That's real good, Mr. Del Rio."

Everybody laughed, and Mr. Del Rio laughed the loudest of all.

"You want some more?" Sam asked. "You can have all you like."

"No, I think that'll do me." Joe still was only able to speak in a whisper. He kept drinking until he had drunk three glasses of water.

After they had eaten their tacos—*without* adding hot sauce—the boys and girls went outside again. "What do you say we look around in some other yards," Joe said.

"We'd better plan this," Juliet said.

"Aw, you always like to make plans," he complained. "Let's just do it."

"No. We've got to be organized," Juliet insisted. And for the next five minutes she talked while the others mostly just listened.

When she was through, Joe said, "So now if you've got the plan made, let's do something." He looked at Sam. "I think she makes a plan every time she takes a bite of food."

"Well, if you had let me plan your famous hot sauce eating, you would have done better. Let's go. It'll be suppertime soon."

4

Another Bike Gone

By the time they had searched the sur-rounding yards, everyone was getting tired of looking. But Juliet said, "Let's see if we can find anything a little farther away—like in empty lots and under bridges."

"That will take forever!" Joe protested. "I'm tired."

"No, it won't. There aren't that many of them around here," Sam said. "I think it's a good idea."

So they split up, Joe and Sam going in one direction, and the three girls going the other way. The search was tiring work, and by the time they had agreed to be back, even Juliet was ready for a break.

"I'd hate to hunt clues for a living," Joe complained.

"You'd hate to do anything for a living except invent things—and eat," Sam teased. "By the way, what invention are you working on now?"

Juliet laughed. "He's trying to make a dumbwaiter."

"What in the world is a dumbwaiter?" Jenny asked.

"Well, we have our bedrooms upstairs, and the kitchen is downstairs," Juliet explained. "So tell them what you want to do, Joe."

"Thomas Jefferson invented the first dumbwaiter. It's a tiny elevator about a foot square, and it goes up and down. For instance, Mom could put our dinner in the dumbwaiter downstairs, ring a bell, and we could pull it up. Then we wouldn't have to go downstairs to eat."

"I wouldn't like that," Sam said. "I like to sit down at the table with the family."

"So do I," Delores agreed. "Family meals are very important to Mexican families."

"They're important to any family, I think," Juliet added. "But you know Joe. He's got his mind set."

"You just wait. You'll like it when it's finished."

On the way home, they planned their strategy for the next day. Juliet thought they should search the nearby park.

Back at the Del Rio house, Mrs. Del Rio greeted them with a smile. "Supper will be ready soon, and your mothers say you may stay. Why don't you girls go up in the attic and play for a while?"

"I'm not going to do that!" Joe said.

"Nobody asked you," Juliet said. "You and Sam stay downstairs. We don't want you, anyhow."

"Yeah, we can play Monopoly," Sam said.

"I don't like Monopoly. You always beat me."

"That's because I'm smarter than you are. Why don't you just start calling me Too Smart Del Rio?"

Juliet sniffed and followed Delores and Jenny upstairs.

The girls always had a fine time trying on old dresses. There were old-fashioned hats in the attic, high-heeled shoes, shawls, and fur coats. It was one of the best places for pretend playing that Juliet had ever found.

They took turns parading in front of the full-length mirror. They pretended to have a tea party, for Mr. Del Rio had put a small table up there and they had cups and saucers. Juliet said, "Maybe we could bring up some real food."

"We'd better not," Delores said. "Grandmother will say we'll spoil our supper."

"I guess she'd be right," Juliet said. "How do you like this outfit?" She had on a pink gown with spangles all over it. It was far too long for her, and it dragged on the floor. She

35

had a feather boa draped around her neck. She'd also found a string of imitation pearls and some rings. On her head was a large hat with an ostrich plume. "How do I look?"

Delores giggled. "You look wonderful. Why don't you wear that to church Sunday?"

After giggling awhile herself, Juliet said, "I wonder what the pastor would think if I dressed up like this and you two wore those things you've got on."

"I bet he couldn't even preach. What was it like back in the olden days when ladies had to wear these clothes?"

"I don't know," Juliet said. "I don't think girls wore anything but dresses then."

"Our people didn't," Delores said. "No woman would be caught dead wearing jeans. And I'll bet your great-grandmother wouldn't have done it, either."

"Things were just different back then. Nothing but long dresses down to your heels and hats with feathers in them."

"But I bet they had fun," Jenny said. "Look how much more fun it is to dress up in these than it is in what we wear."

"I bet someday there'll be girls dressing up in the clothes that *we* wear," Juliet said, "and they'll be talking about how much more fun it is to wear jeans than what they're wearing."

"What do you think they *will* be wearing?" Delores asked.

And then old Mrs. Del Rio came up to interrupt them. "Guess what, girls! You all are spending the night."

"Everybody?" Juliet exclaimed.

"Everybody. The boys and you and Jenny too. I called back your parents, and they've given their permission."

The girls squealed, for they liked nothing better than to have sleep overs.

"Come on down now. It's time for supper."

And what a supper it was. There were enchiladas and tacos and fajitas and tamales, all spicy and delicious. There was a large pitcher of lemonade plus all kinds of soft drinks.

Joe paused once in his eating just long enough to sigh and say, "I wish I could eat a supper like this every night."

"Don't they ever feed you at home?" Sam asked.

"Oh, sure! Our mom's a great cook. But this is a different kind of food."

"Not everybody likes Mexican cooking," Grandfather Del Rio said. "They say it's too hot and spicy." His eyes twinkled, and he picked up the bottle of hot sauce. "Here, Joe. Have some more of this hot sauce you like so much."

Everyone laughed, and even Joe grinned feebly. "I'll pass this time, but I sure like everything else."

They started to talk about different kinds of food.

Mrs. Del Rio said, "Now, I like Chinese food very much!"

"We go out to eat at Hunan's almost every week," Grandfather Del Rio told them. "We all ought to go together sometime."

"But not tonight," Sam said. "Besides, we've got to go put up the tents."

That was the end of the supper, and the boys went out into the backyard to work on the tents with Mr. Del Rio's help. The Del Rios had two good-sized tents. One was already set up as a playhouse for Sam and Delores. The other one went up quickly, and then Mr. Del Rio brought out three cots.

Sam said, "I guess you girls will want to use the cots instead of sleeping on the ground."

"Yes, we do!" Jenny said. "There might be a snake or a scorpion or something else bad!"

Joe looked at her with a frown, then turned to Samuel. "Uh—have you got any more cots, Sam?"

"Oh, yeah. We've got two more, but we've never had any snakes."

"You can't be too careful. Maybe I'll invent an antisnake device."

After dark Mr. Del Rio came out again to build a campfire for them. Everybody sat around it, toasting marshmallows and telling scary stories.

Mr. Del Rio stayed long enough to tell a

scary story himself. His story was the scariest of all. When he came to the end of it, he suddenly yelled and jumped at them, frightening everybody half out of their wits.

"Wow, I guess you're the champion ghost-story teller, Mr. Del Rio," Joe said. "I nearly jumped out of my skin."

"That is the point of ghost stories. They're supposed to make you scared."

"Well, let's cook some more marshmallows," Joe said.

"More marshmallows! How can you eat any more after all the marshmallows you've eaten already?" Juliet protested.

Just then she heard the phone ring, and soon Mrs. Del Rio came to the door. "Telephone for you, Juliet. It's Flash Gordon."

"Oh! OK, I'll be right in."

Juliet went inside, picked up the phone, and said, "Hello, Flash."

"Hi, Juliet. What are you doing over there? I called your house."

"We're having a sleep over."

"Oh. Well, they're always fun. Hey, Juliet, did you hear about Jack Tanner?"

"No, but Jenny's here with us."

Jenny and Jack were now brother and sister, because her widowed mother had married Jack's dad.

"I'll bet she doesn't know this."

"Know what?"

"Somebody stole Jack's bike. And, boy, is he ever mad."

"I can't believe it. That makes four or five bicycles that have been stolen. When was it taken?"

"I don't know for sure. He just called me and told me it was gone. Could hardly talk, he was so mad."

"Flash, we're organizing tomorrow to look for clues for all these missing bicycles. Can you meet us at one o'clock and bring any of our group you can?"

"Well, I can bring Chili for sure—and maybe Billy Rollins."

"Oh. Billy Rollins wouldn't come. And he wouldn't be any good if he did."

"Oh, I don't know. Maybe we need to include Billy. He's really an unhappy guy."

"He's such a . . . a nerd."

"So am I. So are you. We're all nerds at times. Billy needs friends. He shows off just to get attention."

Juliet hesitated. She knew she had said all these things herself at one time or another. "I guess you're right. You always are about people. Go ahead and ask him. And we'll see you tomorrow."

When she went back out to the tent, she said, "Jenny, I've got bad news."

"What is it?"

"Someone stole Jack's bike."

"Oh no! He loved that bike. When?"

"Flash didn't know, but it must have just happened."

Jenny said, "That's just one more bike gone. What is going on?"

Mr. Del Rio went inside, and the youngsters sat around the campfire just talking. Juliet leaned back and clasped her knees, listening to the sounds of the night. She could hear owls hooting and crickets trilling, and finally a huge bullfrog began croaking down at a pond somewhere.

"It's fun being up late like this and out close to the country. We don't get to hear these country sounds where we live."

"You'd get to hear them if you lived here. That bullfrog drives me crazy. He'd better watch out. People say frog legs are good to eat."

"They are," Jenny said. "I've eaten frog legs. They're really good."

"What do they taste like?" Joe asked curiously.

"Sort of like chicken, I guess. Anyway, they're good to eat."

Finally they grew quiet, and Juliet began thinking about bed. "I guess we'd better go to sleep," she said. "We'll have a big day tomorrow, looking for clues."

The three girls went inside their tent and lay down on their cots. It was a mild night, so

Juliet just pulled the sheet up over her. She lay with her head sunk into the pillow, thinking how good the Lord was to let her do fun things like this.

And then she thought she could hear the sound of footsteps. *Who could that be at this time of night?* she wondered.

Quietly she climbed out of the cot and slipped on her sneakers. The girls had not undressed, so she walked all the way out to the street. She looked up and down, but she saw nothing. Overhead an owl swooped down close and said, *"Whoo!"*

"It's me," Juliet told him. "And I guess I'm the only one here." As she started back toward the tent, she muttered, "I don't know what's the matter with me. I'm hearing footsteps when there isn't anybody there. Maybe Billy Rollins is right. I *am* getting too caught up with solving mysteries."

She saw that the other girls were still fast asleep. Too Smart Jones got into her cot, pulled up the sheet, closed her eyes, and went to sleep almost at once.

5

The Stranger

The homeschoolers met by the pond in the park. The group today included Billy Rollins and Jack Tanner, who sometimes hung out together. Jack was a shy boy who was impressed with Billy's loudness. Silently they listened to Juliet explain her plan for discovering something more about the bicycle thieves.

"Now, it's getting cloudy," she said. "I don't know how much time we'll have to look."

"It's not going to rain," Billy announced.

"How do you know?" Sam Del Rio demanded. "Are you a weatherman?"

"Sure. Don't you remember when we went to the TV station? I was the star of the weather program."

"I don't remember anything like that," Sam replied. "It was Flash who was the star."

Billy shook his head. "It's not going to rain. You can take my word for it."

"Well, we don't have time to argue about whether it's going to rain or not," Juliet said. "Here's what we're going to do. I've drawn a map here, and I've broken it down into sections. See? We'll go in teams. Two and two."

"Flash and I'll be one team." Chili took their map, studied it, and handed it to Flash. "I bet we find bicycle thieves all over the place."

"No doubt about it. Let's get started."

The others divided up into pairs. That left Juliet taking both Jenny and Delores with her.

The girls studied their map, and Jenny said, "Do you really think we'll find anything?"

"You never know, Jenny."

"It seems like if the thieves were smart enough to steal bicycles, they'd be smart enough not to leave any clues behind."

"Criminals never think they leave clues behind, but they always do. Chief Bender told me that. He said that you can *always* find a clue if you look for it long enough—and if you look in the right places."

Jenny suddenly laughed. "I bet when you grow up you'll be police chief here in Oakwood."

Actually Juliet had dreams of being police chief in New York City, but she knew that Jenny and Delores would only laugh if she told them. So she did not say anything at all.

The girls looked under two bridges, around

bushes, and behind empty buildings. Several times Juliet tried to get inside old buildings, but they were all locked.

"Maybe we could get in a window," Jenny suggested.

"That would be against the law. You know we can't do that."

"I suppose not." Jenny shrugged. "But if we could just get into some of these places, we might find lots of bikes that the thieves are hiding inside."

"Maybe, but we'll have to find another way."

When Juliet decided that they could do no more, they went back to the Del Rios'. The boys also returned with nothing to report. After a time the girls went up to the attic to play dress up again.

Downstairs the boys got into a fierce game of Monopoly. Before long, Jack Tanner began winning, and Billy Rollins began losing. Billy became more irritable as time went on. And then he landed on one of Jack's pieces of property with a hotel on it.

"I quit!" Billy said. He got up and walked out of the room.

"Aw, come on back, Billy! It's only a game," Jack said.

Then they heard him bang the back door. He was probably going home.

"Not to him it isn't just a game," Sam re-marked. "He can't stand to lose."

"Well," Jack said, "nobody likes to lose."

"But if you make winning the only thing, then playing the game's not much fun," Joe said. "I just like to play the game itself. Some-times I win, sometimes I lose."

"Who was that coach that said it doesn't matter whether you win or lose, it's how you play the game?" Flash wanted to know.

"I don't know, but I agree with him," Joe said.

"Well, Billy doesn't." Sam looked toward the door.

Flash studied the Monopoly board. "I feel sorry for Billy, but someday he's got to learn that there are other people in the world be-sides him."

"I think his only real friends are the Boyd twins, and they're just about as messed up as he is,"Joe said.

Helen and Ray Boyd were identical twins. They always had the most expensive toys, but somehow they also seemed some of the most discontented youngsters around.

Flash said, "Here the richest kids in our group are Billy and the Boyd kids, and they're the ones that are the most unhappy."

"I don't understand that," Sam said. "They can have any toy they want."

"Yeah, they could have about anything, I

guess, if they begged hard enough for it," Joe said thoughtfully.

"I guess it proves that money doesn't make you happy," Flash said. "Well, let's get on with this game before it's time to go."

Just before they all left for home, Juliet said, "I probably should tell you something—I thought I heard something last night."

"Girls! What did you hear?" Flash grinned. "Probably a cricket in your tent."

"No, it wasn't that," Juliet shook her head. "I thought I heard footsteps."

The boys just laughed, and it was her own brother, Joe, who said, "In the middle of the night? No way. That's just your imagination again."

Apparently Jenny did not think so. "You probably did hear *something*, Juliet. What you ought to do is write down exactly what you heard and where it was coming from."

The group broke up and started for home then, but Juliet did not forget what Jenny had said.

When Juliet and Joe got to their study room the next morning, she sat at her desk and just looked around for a time. It was a wonderful room, lined with completed projects such as Joe's Eiffel Tower and his model of a spaceship. Juliet's contributions were colorful drawings and several things that she had woven on her hand loom.

She began drumming on the top of her desk with her fingers. "I can't think, Joe," she said.

"What? Too Smart Jones can't think! Let me call the newspaper! It'll be on the front page!"

"I mean it. All this stuff about bicycles. It just keeps running through my head, and I can't understand it."

"Well, let me give you something else to run through your head. Look at this math problem. It says if a train leaves Chicago at two o'clock and travels sixty miles an hour and another leaves Los Angeles at four o'clock and travels thirty miles an hour . . ."

"Joe, I've showed you how to do those problems over and over again!"

"Well, I think it's dumb. I mean, who needs to know when trains are going to meet? People don't even ride trains anymore. Why don't they do it with airplanes?"

"People do ride trains. And besides, it would be all the same with planes. You just have to learn how to solve problems like that. You have to learn how to think, Joe."

"Think! What do you mean think!" He waved his arms around. "You think the person that made all these projects and inventions can't think?"

"I know you think, Joe, but you want to take shortcuts. You want to know math without learning how to do numbers. You have to start at the beginning."

"That takes too long!"

"Everything you learn that's worthwhile takes time at the beginning. Look how long it's taken us to get where we are with piano lessons. Remember how boring practice was when we first started?"

"That's different. I knew I'd get to play the piano someday if I stayed with it. But what about all this stuff about trains? I'm not going to run a train station. Ever."

"It's just practice! And you need the practice!"

They were still arguing when the door opened and their mother came in. "What in the world are you two fussing about?"

"About these dumb problems. Why do I have to do them?"

"In order to become educated. Now, I came up to give you some additional work."

Joe groaned and pulled his hair. "Additional work! I can't do what I've got now."

Mrs. Jones, however, ignored his protests. She gave them each more math problems, and Juliet knew hers were far more difficult than Joe's.

"Now if you get through these and do your chores, I'll have a reward for you."

"The only reward you can give me is to burn this math book," Joe muttered.

"What did you say, Joe?"

"Oh, nothing, Mom. Just mumbling to myself."

In the afternoon, the homeschoolers met in a park on the other side of town from where the Joneses lived. Juliet did not know this territory well.

Chili and Flash were playing a game of basketball when she and Joe arrived, and Chili was taking a little ribbing because Flash was beating him at "horse." Flash would wheel his chair to different spots on the court, throw the ball, and make every basket. Chili would stand in the same spot as Flash had and try the same shot. Chili missed about as many shots as he made. He was definitely losing this game.

Losing didn't seem to bother Chili, though. He said, "I'll beat him next time. I just ate lunch, and I'm too full to give the game my all."

"You sound like Billy," Flash told him. "Billy, what's your excuse?"

"Excuse for what?" Billy asked. "I'm not even in the game!"

Juliet interrupted. "Listen, we haven't got time to argue about games. Let's sit down here on these benches and plan where we're going to start looking."

Once again, she had drawn maps, and Billy groaned when he saw them. "Why do we need a map? Let's just go out and start looking."

"That's the way Joe does his homework. He doesn't want to get any basics done. Now, look. We know that there are people stealing bicycles, and Chief Bender says that criminals always leave clues. All we've got to do is find a clue."

After some more argument, the group split up, and the search was on. This time all the boys went in one direction and the girls in another.

Chili and Flash went together. As usual, Flash was sailing along in his wheelchair. Chili trotted at his side.

"There's an old jogging path. Let's check it out. It's smooth enough for your wheelchair."

"Sounds like a winner!"

So the two boys took a worn trail that was used by walkers and joggers and bike riders. After a while, Flash said, "I see something over there!"

"Where?"

"There. Right over there. See?"

Chili trotted over to where Flash pointed and picked up a piece of metal. "Looks like part of an old bicycle."

"Huh! Wonder what *that's* doing here in the park?"

"It's all rusty. Probably somebody just threw it away. Doesn't look like it has anything to do with all these stealings."

Joe and Samuel turned off on a well-kept park trail.

"Look there. It's some bicycle tracks," Joe said.

Sam gave the tracks only a quick look. "Yeah, there's always bicycle tracks along here. Bikers use it all the time. I sure don't know what we can hope to find."

"Oh, well, you know my sister. She says we've got to find clues. So we'll look for clues."

Juliet and the other girls checked around the baseball diamond, the tennis area, and the basketball courts. Although they had a good time looking, they found nothing of interest.

Finally the boys and girls met back at the pond.

"So what did the rest of you find out?" Juliet asked the boys.

"The same thing you found out," Billy Rollins said, disgusted. "Nothing."

Juliet questioned everybody carefully and was disappointed to learn that Billy was right. "Well, let's go back," she said. "I think we earned ourselves a treat. How about ice cream?"

"Sure, I'll have rocky road," Flash said. "Come on!" He wheeled his chair along, and soon the others were straining to keep up with him.

"It's wonderful how he can make that thing go so fast!" Juliet panted to Jenny, who was running beside her.

"He must have arms like iron. I tried wheeling a wheelchair once, and my arms didn't last any time at all."

Back in town, they wound their way through the streets toward the ice cream shop.

All of a sudden Juliet stopped them and stood stock-still. "Look coming," she said.

Sam said, "Why? Nobody I ever saw before."

They were looking at a teenage boy who was pushing a bicycle along. As he drew closer, Juliet saw that the front tire was flat.

When he got near enough, she said, "Hi."

The stranger stopped and looked at them. He had long stringy hair and a baseball cap on backwards. He wore a bulky long-sleeved shirt and a pair of faded jeans. "Hi," he said. "What kind of a bunch are you?"

"Oh, we're all in school together."

"Which school?"

"Different ones. Our parents teach us. We're homeschoolers."

The boy laughed. He had a wide mouth, and his eyes were half hidden by heavy eyelids. "Well, that beats going to the school I went to—when I went."

"Aren't you in school now?" Sam asked cautiously.

"Nah! Not me. Got other things to do."

"Where you going with the bike?" Joe asked.

"I was just riding around and had a flat."

Juliet said, "My name's Juliet Jones. These are all my friends. I don't guess we ever met you."

"No, you never did."

Juliet noticed that the boy didn't give his name.

"You need some help getting that flat fixed?" Sam asked.

"Nah, I can take care of it. So long now."

"Do you live around here?"

The boy stopped and took his cap off. His hair fell over his eyes, and he pushed it back. "My grandmother lives here. I brought this bike along on a visit. Don't know anybody else in town. Don't much want to, either."

With that, he moved off, walking fast and pushing the bike in front of him. They looked after him until he turned into an alley and disappeared.

"What kind of a guy is that, I wonder," Jenny said. "He didn't act like he trusts many people."

"He looked suspicious to me," Juliet said. Suddenly she grabbed her notebook out of her backpack and began scribbling.

"What are you writing in that book?" Billy asked.

"I'm writing down that boy's description. And a description of the bike. And the way he was headed."

"Well, he looked pretty dirty all right, but that's not against the law," Billy said. "If you put dirty people in jail, you'd put old Joe Jones in. Right, Joe? I heard you haven't had a bath since spring."

Joe was used to Billy's kind of humor.

"I've had as many baths as you have. Now let's go get that ice cream."

6

The Alley

When Juliet joined her family for breakfast the following morning, she found her father talking about a newspaper article.

"It says that there's been a rash of bicycle thefts in town lately," Mr. Jones was saying.

"Daddy, let me see that!"

Juliet usually tried to be polite, but this time, without thinking, she jerked the newspaper out of her father's hand. She read the headlines and then looked up to see him staring at her. "Oh, I'm sorry, Daddy. I didn't mean to do that." She handed the paper back, and her father raised one eyebrow but said no more.

Joe said, "It looks like Too Smart Jones is going to be right for once. I laughed at her about being too suspicious, but bicycles are disappearing all over town."

"Four or five kids that we know have lost theirs," Juliet said.

"You'd better take care of yours, Joe," Mrs. Jones said. "Sometimes you can be careless."

"Don't worry about that. I will."

"I see that Chief Bender thinks a gang of young hoodlums is stealing bicycles and taking them to another town to sell them. There may even be a thievery ring all over the country."

"Oh, this is really big, isn't it?" Juliet said excitedly.

When they had thanked the Lord for their food, she picked up her fork. "I think what we ought to do—" she began.

"Stop right there, Juliet!" Mr. Jones said. "This case is too big for you."

"But, Dad, somebody's got to find out—"

"That's a job for the police."

"Your father's right, dear," Mrs. Jones said. "Besides, this could be dangerous. You stay out of it."

"But, Mom, we're not really doing anything."

"That's what *you* say," Joe complained. "I'm sore all over. She's had us looking all over town for clues."

Juliet tried to convince her parents, but in the end they made it plain that this was police business and she was to let the police take care of it.

"I'm going to keep *my* bike locked on the

front porch," Joe announced. "Nobody's going to steal my mountain bike!"

"You worked hard for that bike, Joe," Mr. Jones said. "So take care of it."

"I saved every bit of my money for a year, and it took a lot of work, I'll tell you!"

Juliet knew that this was true, and she had seen how Joe treasured his bicycle. He took very good care of it. That was the one chore that he never had to be told to do. She watched him shovel in his scrambled eggs and said, "You sure do like to eat, Joe."

"Who doesn't?"

"You should see him eat Mrs. Del Rio's Mexican food," Juliet told their parents. "He likes it all—except for the hot sauce."

"Never mind about the hot sauce!"

Their dad grinned. "What did he do? Get a little bit too much?"

"He looked like a thermometer. His face got all red, and I thought his brains were going to be blown out of his ears."

"You be quiet, Juliet!"

"He doesn't like to talk about it, but everybody teases him every time we eat there."

"I just got a little bit too much that one time. That's all."

"Well, one drop of some of that Mexican hot sauce is too much for me," Mr. Jones said.

"And what are you two up to today?" their mother asked.

"Just having fun. Saturday is my favorite day," Joe said.

After breakfast, they unlocked their bikes and started out. They decided just to ride around for a while and see if they could find anybody who wanted to play soccer or pick-up basketball.

"There come Jenny and Chili. And they're both on bikes. Where did he get that one?"

Chili's bicycle proved to be one that he had when he was younger, and it was too small for him. "This is from one of the seven dwarfs," he grumbled. "I can't believe I was ever so little that this was too big for me."

"Well, let's race," Juliet said. "I think I can beat you on that one."

The four took off, and, as usual, Joe won. Jenny came in second, Juliet third, and Chili for once was last. "I'm going to junk this thing!" he said.

"There comes Sam! Look at what he's riding. It's worse than yours, Chili."

Sam Del Rio, Juliet saw, rode a rusty old bicycle with a front wheel so wobbly that he could hardly stay on.

"Just look at this," he complained.

Juliet could tell that Sam was very upset. *I guess I'd feel the same way,* she thought, *if I lost my good bicycle and had to ride this.*

"At least you've got wheels again. Let's ride through town." She led the way down the main street. And then they came to an alley. It was the alley the strange boy had turned into yesterday —the one whose bicycle had a flat.

"Why are you slowing down here?" Sam asked.

"Oh, I don't know."

"I do," Joe said. "It's where we saw that guy go yesterday."

"Well, that's right," Juliet admitted. "I was just thinking about it."

"Thinking about what?" Jenny asked. "Do you think he's a suspect?"

"I don't know. Probably not."

As they rode on, Juliet's eyes took in everything. She saw the large doors where the shopkeepers had their wares delivered. She saw the back doors to the apartments located on top of the shops. She looked at some empty garages with black paint covering their windows. She was about ready to turn around and go back when she caught sight of something interesting.

"Why are you stopping?" Chili called out.

"I just want to see what this is."

Juliet slid off the bike and picked up a piece of shiny metal. "See!"

"That's a luggage carrier. Somebody's lost it off his bike," Sam replied.

"He'll want it back," Juliet said. "It looks new."

The group gathered around to get a look. And then they headed back up the street.

They were passing the alley again when Juliet thought she heard something. She put a finger to her lips and said, "Just a minute. Let me listen. I think I hear something."

Everybody waited, quiet and still, and then Sam said, "I think I hear it, too. It's voices."

"Yeah—coming from down the alley," Jenny said.

"Let's get closer."

Juliet thought it sounded like the excited voices of boys. And they seemed to be coming from somewhere deep inside the empty building at the corner of the alley.

She got off her bike and tried the building's front door. It was locked. She said, "I wish we could see who's back in there."

"Well, we're not likely to unless we knock the door down and march right in," Chili said. "Do you want to do that?"

"No, I don't. Well, let's go on."

But before Too Smart Jones got on her bicycle, she whipped out her notebook and wrote down everything she could think of.

"You still want to keep this luggage carrier?" Joe asked.

"Yes. Bring it along. We might see the owner looking for it. Or it might be a clue."

"Everything's a clue," Joe complained. But he got on his bike and led the way home.

7

A Job for
the Police

Juliet came awake when something suddenly
touched her lips. She uttered a little scream
and sat straight up in bed.

She'd been dreaming about bicycles. It had
been a strange dream, too. She seemed to see
hundreds of bicycles moving down the streets
of Oakwood and past her house. The strangest
thing was that no one was riding them. They
kept coming by and coming by in greater
numbers. They came in all colors—red and
green and pink and purple. There was something frightening about the fact that the pedals
turned and the wheels rolled and, when they
approached a corner, the handlebars turned. It
was as though hundreds of mysterious riders
were on hundreds of ghostly bicycles.

It was already light outside, and the sunlight streamed through the windows onto her bed. There, sitting in her lap, was her kitten.

"Boots, I wish you wouldn't do that! You scared me."

Boots looked up at her, said, *"Mrow!"* then began to lick the fur on his chest. Juliet picked him up and began to stroke his silky fur. The cat had four perfectly white feet. Because she had gotten him for her last birthday, he was especially precious to her. She began to talk to him, as she often did when nobody else was around.

"Boots," she murmured, "I'm thinking too much about bicycles. I was even dreaming about them just before you woke me up."

Boots did not seem to find bicycles very interesting. He began to paw at a button on the front of Juliet's pajamas. Then he leaped up onto her shoulder. His claws dug in, and she yelped, "Ouch, don't do that!" She pulled him loose and dropped him to the floor.

Boots began to run about the room. Seemingly, just running gave him great pleasure. Around and around he went, under the bed, up on the chair, over the desk, and then back to pounce on Juliet again. This time he sank his claws into her knee.

She picked him up, held him high, and shook him. "Don't do that, Boots!" she said. "You don't know how sharp those claws are!"

He went limp, as he did sometimes, and

she held him close as she would a tiny baby. "But you're such a nice cat," she whispered. "You're just more fun than any other cat could ever be."

At that moment she heard a sound from downstairs, and she put Boots down. "That's Mom starting breakfast," she said. "Now I've got to get dressed and go help her."

It was Sunday, and she dressed quickly, choosing a new outfit. It was a navy blue dress with diagonal stripes, and she liked it very much. Her father had helped her pick it out, and that made it extraspecial. She slipped on her black patent leather shoes and quickly brushed her hair.

She found her mother in the kitchen, beginning to put breakfast together.

"Let me help, Mom."

"All right. We're going to have omelets this morning."

"Oh boy! Everybody likes omelets!" Juliet said. "Can we have different kinds?"

"We're going to," Mrs. Jones said. "What kind would you like?"

"I like omelet with chopped ham in it."

"Well, you can work on that while I fix your father's and mine. He wants everything but the kitchen sink in his."

"And Joe likes onions and garlic in his. Ugh!"

"That's what he likes, so that's what he gets

since it's going to be a special Sunday morning breakfast."

Juliet cracked two eggs into a bowl and added a little milk. Then she took a wire whip and beat the mixture. After that she took a thin slice of ham, cut it into small pieces, and added it to the beaten eggs. Finally she shook in a dash of salt and pepper.

By the time the omelets were all ready and the Texas toast was nice and buttery and crisp, Joe and Mr. Jones were coming into the kitchen.

Joe sniffed the air. "What's that I smell? Could it be omelets?"

"It's omelets," his mother said with a smile. "You've been such a good boy lately that I think you deserve a special treat, so I made you an oversized omelet."

Joe gaped at the huge omelet that filled his plate, and he cried, "That makes my mouth water!"

"Well, let's sit down," Mr. Jones said. "We have a visiting speaker this morning, and he might preach a long sermon. So let's all get ready for it."

The family held hands, and Mr. Jones prayed. "Lord, we thank You for this food. We thank You for the night's rest. We thank You for this beautiful morning. You have been so good to us, Lord, and we're grateful for every favor. Now please guide us and watch over us. In Jesus' name. Amen."

"Amen," everybody echoed, and then Mr. Jones said, "All right, Joe, lay your ears back and fly right at it."

Joe needed no encouragement, nor did the others. They all liked omelets, and for a while there was not much talk while breakfast went on.

When Joe managed to put away the last of his giant omelet, he patted his stomach. "I'm about as full as it's possible to be. I don't think I can stay awake at church."

"Yes, you will, or I'll pinch you," his mother threatened cheerfully. "I remember when you were very young and you wouldn't behave. I couldn't spank you in church, so I'd just pinch you."

Joe laughed. "I remember that! You sure were mean to me."

"She was never mean to you!" Juliet told him. "She did the same thing to me, and we both deserved it."

"I'm glad to hear all these confessions." Mr. Jones got up and pushed his chair under the table. "Now let's get ourselves ready."

Ten minutes later they were out in the car. Mr. Jones had just bought a Bronco, which the family liked very much, even though it was not brand-new. They had had a *very* old car before, one that especially Joe hated. In a minute more the Joneses were happily rolling along to church.

As everyone piled out onto the church parking lot, Mr. Jones shook his finger at Juliet and Joe. "You kids had better hurry, or you'll be late for Sunday school."

"All right, Dad. We'll see you in church," Juliet said.

The two sped off to their Sunday school room and found that most of the class was already there.

Chili Williams grinned at them as they came in. "And here comes the great detective Sherlock Jones and her assistant. How's it going?"

"Great, Chili," Joe said. "Why don't you come over this afternoon, and we'll play some more Monopoly."

"Sounds all right to me."

At that moment in came Billy Rollins. Usually Billy charged into Sunday school hollering or pushing or making a general nuisance out of himself. But this morning he did no such thing. In fact, there was a sad, long look on his face. He just walked over to a chair and plumped himself down.

Ray Boyd asked, "What's the matter, Billy?"

"Nothing."

"There must be something," Helen Boyd said. "You look terrible."

Listening to this conversation, Juliet too wondered what was the matter with Billy. He usually was so unbearable that she stayed as far away from him as possible, but this time she saw that he was really upset about something. "What's the matter, Billy? Are you sick?"

"No, I'm not sick. Just let me alone."

"You can tell us," Juliet urged. "We're all friends in here. Before Mr. Blanton comes in, just let us know what's wrong."

Billy Rollins bit his lip and ran his hands through his hair. "I couldn't believe it would happen to me," he muttered.

"Believe what happened to you?" Flash Gordon asked. He moved his wheelchair a little closer and reached over and put a hand on Billy's shoulder. "Come on, fella, we're all friends here. What's wrong?"

Billy looked up at Flash, and for a moment it seemed he would say nothing. But then he burst out, "Somebody stole my brand-new bike, that's what's wrong! It wasn't even a month old."

"Stole your bike!" Flash exclaimed. "You too?"

"Yes, me too. I couldn't believe it."

"How did it happen? Tell us!" Juliet cried. She suddenly was very sorry for Billy Rollins. She knew he felt terrible.

At that moment their teacher came in. "I'm sorry to be late, class. You shouldn't have to wait for me," he said. "Well, let's get right down to the Sunday school lesson."

"Mr. Blanton, can we put off the Sunday school lesson a little?" Juliet asked earnestly.

"What for?" he asked with great surprise.

"We—we have a big problem here. Several of our class have had their bicycles stolen. Samuel has lost his, and Chili, and now someone's taken Billy's. He just came in and told us."

"Is that right?" Mr. Blanton said. "I've been reading about a rash of bicycle thefts, but I didn't know any of you had lost bikes."

"Come on, Billy. Tell us how it happened," Samuel urged.

"Well, I always kept my bike inside the garage. You know we have a garage with an opener on it. All you have to do is punch a button in the car, and it goes up." He shook his head back and forth. "Nobody can figure out how they got that bicycle out of there. How could anybody do that if they didn't have a door opener?"

"Well, there's another door to the garage, isn't there?" Juliet asked. "Somebody could have gotten in that way."

"Sure. There's a door over to the side, but it was locked! It's like that bicycle just—vanished. We don't know how they got in, but somebody did."

"Did you have the bike locked?" Chili asked.

"Not with a chain, if that's what you mean. But it was gone when I went out to get it this morning." Tears came into Billy's eyes. "My folks gave it to me. It was my early Christmas present. And now it's gone."

"They can get you another one," Jack Tanner said. Everybody knew Billy's parents had money to buy things. Perhaps Jack thought saying that might help.

"No. It's not the same thing. You know how you get used to things, and you like them. Well, that bicycle was real special to me. My dad picked it out himself."

And Juliet knew just how he felt. She had some things that were very special to her. She said, "I'm really sorry, Billy."

"Me too," Jenny White said. "It's just awful to lose something like that."

Mr. Blanton listened for a while and then said, "I think we ought to pray right now for those who have lost their bicycles. God is able to bring them back, you know—or to do something even better than that. That's the way it is when we have troubles. Troubles are to teach us something."

This seemed to cheer Billy a little. And maybe it helped that the class members were so kind to him. He looked around as if he were seeing them for the first time. "Well, thanks, you guys," he mumbled. "It's . . . it's . . . it's nice to have friends."

"Sure," Flash said. "We're all in this thing together."

Mr. Blanton prayed then, and they began the Sunday school lesson.

On the way home after church, Joe and

71

Juliet sat in the backseat of the Bronco and talked about what had happened.

Joe said, "I never saw Billy act like that. He's usually a pain in the neck!"

"What's that about Billy?" their father asked.

"Well, somebody stole his bicycle, too."

"And he came into class looking like a bad accident had happened," Juliet said.

"That's terrible!" Mrs. Jones said. "This bicycle thing is getting out of hand completely!"

"That hits a little close to home," Mr. Jones agreed. "Was the bicycle outside?"

"No! It was locked in the garage, and it took the door opener to open the door."

Juliet's dad listened to them talk about the missing bicycles until they pulled into the driveway at home. As soon as they were inside, he said, "We're going to have to do something about this. I don't know who's stealing bicycles, but these could be dangerous people."

"What are you going to do, Dad?" Juliet asked. "You said it was a job for the police."

"It is. But we're going to help. I'm going to call all the parents around here, and we're going to have a neighborhood watch."

"Ooh, that's great, Dad!" Juliet cried. "Can I be in charge of it?"

Mr. Jones gave her a hug, but he said, "No, I think this is more of a grown-up thing. But I'm sure you can be involved in the watching."

Juliet felt a little put out at that. After all, she had been investigating the case already. "But I want to do more than just be 'involved in watching.'"

"We know." Joe grinned at her. "You want to be in charge."

"Well, there's no way you can be in charge of this," Mr. Jones said firmly. "This is grown-up work."

Suddenly Joe got up. "I think I'll go out and make sure that my bike is locked up."

While he was doing that, Juliet was begging her father to let her do more than just a little watching.

"Dad, I want to help, and I think I've got some ideas on how to find out who this is."

"Not this time, Juliet. I know you like to go around working on mysteries, but this could be dangerous. As I keep saying, this is a grown-up problem."

When her father spoke so positively, Juliet knew that was the end of it, so she gave up coaxing. But just the same, she kept thinking about the neighborhood watch.

She heard him on the phone, calling different parents. Late that afternoon he came into the family room to announce, "We're going to have a meeting before church. I think we can get to the bottom of this if we all co-operate."

"Can I go to the meeting?" Juliet asked.

"No, Juliet, you can't."

"Aw, Dad, let me go! Please!"

"No, it's a meeting for the parents, and that's final."

By now, Juliet was beginning to feel a bit persecuted. She went off to her room, sat at her desk, and began to write in her journal. She wrote:

Dear Journal, I don't think it's fair. I've been the one who's been investigating this bicycle stealing. And now that the grown-ups are actually going to do something about it, Dad won't let me have anything to do with it. Looks like grown-ups just don't care about kids anymore.

For a moment Juliet sat looking at what she had written. Then she leaned forward and began to write again:

I've just read what I wrote, and it sounds whiny! I've been feeling sorry for myself, and I'm always wanting to be in charge of every-thing. That's wrong, and I need to work on it. So I'm going to ask the Lord to help me be more willing to just be one of the bunch in-stead of being a leader every single time.

When Juliet put the journal away, she felt much better about the neighborhood meeting.

"There," she said aloud, "that's another reso-
lution, and I hope I can keep it." She looked
down at Boots. The cat was chewing on her
slipper, and she sighed. "Boots, I wish I didn't
have any more problems than you have. As
long as you have some tuna fish and something to play with, you're happy."

Boots looked up and said, *"Mrow!"* After
that he went back to chewing on the slipper.

8

More Clues

When Juliet came to the breakfast table the following morning, the first thing she asked her father was, "Did you get all of the plans made for the neighborhood watch?"

"Yes, we did," Mr. Jones said. He sat down and began sipping the coffee that he had brought to the table while they were waiting for breakfast. "Apparently the neighborhood watch idea has caught on over the whole town. People are going to take turns in different neighborhoods. My turn here will be from seven to nine tomorrow night."

"Boy, that's a big job!" Juliet said.

"It is, but sooner or later we're going to catch the thieves, whoever they are. If they're still operating around here."

"But if you see a little kid just riding a bicycle, what would you do? You wouldn't know whether it was a bicycle they'd stolen or whether it was theirs."

"Juliet, I don't think it's *kids* that are stealing these bicycles. I think it will be someone a little older." Mr. Jones took another sip of coffee and added some sugar. "It won't be easy. We'll just have to keep our eyes open and pay special attention to anyone who acts suspicious in any way."

"Can I go with you when you're on your watch?"

"I don't see why you couldn't do that. If you want to."

"Oh, good!"

Juliet suddenly felt much better. Now she felt that she was going to play an active part in the watching. She helped her mother get breakfast ready.

When Juliet finished her after-breakfast chores, she went upstairs to find Joe already working on his model of the Empire State Building. He loved to do models, and this one was going to be his masterpiece, he said. He said so again as he looked up and saw her come in.

"I'd like to enter this thing in some contest," he said. "I'll bet it'd win first place."

"It's a beauty," Juliet admitted. She came over to admire his work. It was made from a kit, but it was very complicated. Joe always worked quickly, and she marveled, "You're so quick with your hands."

"I guess all my brains are in my hands." He grinned and added another piece. "I'd rather have them in my head."

"You've got plenty of brains! You're just too lazy to use them, and you always want to take shortcuts for everything."

"Well, I'm in a hurry to get things done. You drive me crazy sometimes, the way you work so slow."

"I just like to do it right, and sometimes the quickest way is the slowest way."

"That sounds like something you read in a book somewhere," Joe teased. He added one more piece. "Uh—why don't you help me on this, and then later on I'll let you help me with my math lesson."

Juliet laughed. "Why don't you just let me do it all?"

"Hey, that's a good idea! I could go over and shoot baskets with Chili, and you could do all the work."

Juliet went over to her desk. "Nope. You're going to have to do your own work." She got busy at once. She was supposed to write a short story, but she soon discovered that she was not particularly good at making up stories. After a while she looked across at Joe and said, "I can't get this story right."

He glued a piece onto the Empire State

Building, then said, "So let me hear what you've got. Read it to me."

Juliet read what she had written, feeling rather self-conscious. When she finished, she said, "It's not very good."

"No, it's sure not."

Juliet felt somewhat irritated at that honest remark. "Well, why don't you give me some ideas, if you think you could do better?"

"Sure. I'll be glad to. Then you can help me with my math."

Joe got up. He began to talk about the story as he walked around.

Juliet was surprised at how imaginative he was. She was better at anything that required reading or careful thinking, but the Lord had given her brother a wildly creative mind. Soon she was jotting down ideas that she could work into her story.

"There,"Joe said. "That ought to be enough for you."

"Let me get all this down. Then I'll help you with your math."

Joe grinned and went back to his desk. "We make a pretty good team, don't we?"

"We sure do. Sometimes."

"Yeah. Sometimes you're a pain in the neck." He shrugged. "But I forgive you."

"Thanks a lot!" She made a face at him.

Juliet worked on her story and then helped

Joe. Later in the morning, their mother came in to check on them.

By now, Juliet was excited. "I want you to hear what I've written, Mom."

"All right. Read it to me." Mrs. Jones took a seat, leaned back, and listened intently as Juliet read the story.

"That's a great story!" she said. "I didn't know you had such a creative mind!"

"She doesn't. I do," Joe said calmly.

"Are you saying you wrote that story, Joe?"

"No. I wrote it, Mom, but he did give me some of the ideas. He's creative, isn't he?"

"Yes, Joe's always had plenty of that in him. If we could just get him to study hard on the little things like adding and subtracting."

"Aw, those are details," Joe said.

Nevertheless, their mother said he had done well on his math—with Juliet's help. She went over all their work, graded it, and said, "You two have done so well that I'm going to give you a reward. You can take the afternoon off!"

"Yeah!" Joe yelled. He got so excited that he almost knocked over the Empire State Building. "Woops," he said. "Don't want to break that. It's going to win first prize in the science fair—or something."

"What are you planning to do for the science fair, Juliet?" Mrs. Jones asked. "Have you given it some thought?"

"I'm not good at making things like Joe is. Maybe I ought to just write something."

"That's no good," Joe said right away. "You need something people can see. Why don't you make a steam engine?"

"I wouldn't know how to do that."

He acted surprised. "It's easy. You just put water in a tank, heat it up, and when the steam comes out, it turns a wheel."

"It sounds hard," Juliet said. "I wouldn't know how to start."

"I'll help you," Joe said importantly. "You'll win first place if you do what I tell you."

"I need to get going on a project all right. Could we start on it this afternoon—before we go and play?"

"We can start right now. The first thing we do is start collecting the materials."

"No, let's make a drawing of it first."

"I don't need a drawing."

"But I do," Juliet said. "I have to see what it looks like, and you'll have to explain to me how it works."

"Oh, all right, then."

Mrs. Jones looked at them fondly. "That sounds good to me," she said. "Now, while you two do that, I'll go make a cake. What kind would you like?"

Juliet and Joe got into an argument about that. Juliet always wanted chocolate, while Joe wanted banana nut.

"I'll make one of each," Mrs. Jones said. "I'm sure that none of it will go to waste around this house."

Juliet and Joe worked on the steam engine project before and after lunch, and Juliet grew very interested in it. Then they decided to take their break.

They went to the garage, unlocked their bikes, and, as usual, had a race—which, also as usual, Juliet lost.

Then Juliet said, "Let's go over to Jenny's house."

"No, let's go over to the Del Rios' house," Joe argued. "They'll give us something to eat."

"But Jenny might have something to eat, too."

"OK. Jenny's first, then Del Rios'."

At Jenny's house they left their bikes by the porch, went up the steps, and knocked.

Jenny herself came to the door, and the first thing she said was, "You won't believe what's happened!" She looked as if she was about to cry. "Somebody stole *my* bike!"

"After all the talk, you left your bike *outside?*"

"It was in the backyard, but we've got a fence all the way around. They would have to climb over the fence and lift the bike over. There's no other way they could have taken it."

"Wait. Wait a minute," Joe said. "Wow. You

only live three blocks away from us. That's getting really close."

Jenny said, "It wasn't a new bike. Dad said he was going to buy me a new one—and Jack too. But I was going to give the old one to a little girl down the street who doesn't have any bike at all."

"Show me where the bike was. We'll look for clues," Juliet said.

Soon the four of them, including Jack by now, were out in the backyard. They had looked around for some time when Juliet went over to the fence. "This part of your yard is really soft."

Jack came up beside her. "It always gets that way when it rains." Then he looked closely at the ground, "Look at that! There's the print of bicycle tires!" He turned and called, "Did you ride your bike over here, Jenny?"

"No, I never had it over there."

Joe joined them, and he said, "There's some footprints too. Do they look like yours, Jack?"

"You think I've got feet that big? And see—whoever it was was wearing boots."

Juliet got down on her hands and knees. "They're Western boots. Look how sharp the heels and toes are."

For a time they examined the prints. Then Juliet said, "Let's make casts of them."

"How do you do that?" Jack asked.

"You mix up plaster of Paris, and you pour it into the prints. When it gets hard, you've got a perfect cast—just the shape of the footprints. Then if you find the person who wore these boots, you'd have a case against them."

"But we don't have any plaster of Paris."

Juliet looked disappointed. "Maybe we could use something else. Something that you could heat up that would turn hard." She thought for a while and then said, "I know. We could melt some wax and pour it into the print and wait until it gets hard and then take it out."

"My mom has lots of pieces of wax," Jenny said. "She puts it on top of her jars when she makes jelly. I'll ask her if we can have some."

Jenny did, and her mother even helped them melt some wax. They made a cast of one good footprint, and Juliet knew that this was a real clue.

"Somebody wears Western boots. Aren't too many people who wear those around here."

"Let's look on the other side of the fence," Jenny suggested.

"That's a good idea."

The four of them trooped around to the far side of the fence. When they got there, Juliet said, "And see, whoever it was rode the bicycle away right here."

There were also more footprints.

"But these aren't Western boots. These are some kind of running shoes. Maybe Nikes."

"Let's make a cast of them too."

After they did, Juliet said, "While the wax gets hard, let's follow the bike tracks."

She noticed that the tracks went off to the west, but they soon lost them. And then Juliet said, "Stop!"

"What is it?" Jenny asked.

"Look here." Juliet picked up a paper.

"What have you got there?" Joe asked, bending close.

"It's another Fudgy candy wrapper just like the one we found over at Sam's house."

Everybody got excited then.

But Jack said, "I never heard of Fudgy candy."

"I hadn't either," Juliet said. "Let's go down to the grocery store and ask Mr. Simpson about it. He's got all kinds of candy there."

They found Mr. Simpson putting out fresh vegetables. He was a tall man with kindly gray eyes and a shock of brown hair. "Well, this looks like a committee coming! What can I do for you folks?"

"Mr. Simpson, have you ever heard of Fudgy candy?"

"You mean the candy bars?"

"That's right."

"Sure, I have," Mr. Simpson said. "You want some? Come on. I'll show you."

He walked over to the cases that held the candy bars and picked up one. "Kind of an unusual wrapper, isn't it?" It was bright red with a gold crown on it. "I think these are made outside the country somewhere. We just got them in recently. Don't seem to sell many."

"Would you know who did buy some of them?"

Mr. Simpson laughed loudly at that. "No way. How would I know that? People go through here by the hundreds."

Juliet was disappointed. "Well, if somebody does come in and buys a lot of them, let me know, will you?"

"What's this all about?"

Juliet did not like to give away secrets about clues. "Oh, we're just curious about . . . something," she said.

"Well, if anybody comes in and buys me out of Fudgy candy bars, I'll be sure to let you know, Juliet."

"Thanks, Mr. Simpson."

They started back to Jenny and Jack's house. On the way, Juliet said, "We're on the right track. We've got some clues now."

"That's right," Joe said with a laugh. "All we have to do is find somebody who wears Western boots and eats Fudgy bars."

Juliet knew he was teasing her. "It's just a start," she said. "But sooner or later we're going to catch whoever is doing this. Let's go back to the store. I think we deserve a reward for being good detectives."

"What are you thinking of?" Jack Tanner asked. "Something to eat?"

"I'd like to have some peanuts," Juliet said. "I get hungry for peanuts."

"You get peanuts, and I'll get Cracker Jacks," Joe said.

Back in Mr. Simpson's store, they bought treats for themselves. Jack Tanner bought a Fudgy bar.

When they were outside again, he stripped off the paper and took a bite. "Yuck!" he said. "This is awful!"

"Let me taste it," Juliet said. She broke off a small piece and found that the chocolate was so strong it almost bit her. She made a face and watched as Joe and Jenny sampled it. Juliet said, "Anybody that would eat these things has to be crazy."

"There can't be too many people who are going to buy Fudgy bars!" Joe said, sounding very sure of himself. "So what we do is keep our eyes open for anybody eating one of these awful things."

Juliet felt they had made progress. She said, "I get to go with Dad on his watch tonight. I'll bet we find whoever this is real quick."

9

The Thieves
Strike Again

uliet and Joe asked their father to come in and look at their work, and after Saturday lunch he did. "Now, what are these exciting projects you've been working on?" he asked.

"You go first, Joe," Juliet said.

"All right," her brother said eagerly. "Look, Dad. The Empire State Building."

"Well, now. Let me see what you've done here. As a professional engineer, my standards are very high, you know."

Joe watched anxiously as his father walked around his project.

The model was five feet high and all the details were there—the windows, the spire on the top, the famous observation deck. Joe had worked hard on it, and he thought it was beautiful.

But his father stroked his chin and did not say anything for a long time.

"What's the matter, Dad? Don't you like it?"

Mr. Jones turned slowly. There was a very serious expression on his face.

Joe looked even more worried. "Is it wrong, Dad? What's the matter? Why don't you say something?"

Mr. Jones just frowned, and Joe looked ready to cry. "But, Dad, I worked on it as hard as I could. I thought it was all right."

"Son . . ." Mr. Jones said, and he continued stroking his chin. It was a habit of his when he was going to make an important announcement. "I will have to say . . ." He paused.

Joe sat down in a chair and stared at his feet. "You don't like it, do you, Dad?"

"I was just going to say . . ." Mr. Jones said slowly—and then he burst out laughing—"that this is about the finest model I have ever seen in my entire life!"

Joe jumped to his feet, his eyes gleaming. "Do you mean it?"

"Of course I mean it. Would I not tell you the truth? I'm an engineer, and I like the good job you've done on the proportions." Mr. Jones talked about the various aspects of the model until Joe was beaming from ear to ear.

Their dad finally said, "If this doesn't win first prize at the science fair, then there's no justice. You've done a fine job, son, and I'm proud of you."

Joe plunked down in his chair and wiped his forehead. "Wow, Dad, I thought you didn't like it. You scared me to death."

"I thought a little anxiety would do you good."

Joe laughed out loud then. "You'd make a good actor, Dad. If you ever stop engineering, you can go in the movies or on TV."

"No, thanks. I'll stick to building bridges and such things." He turned to Juliet. "Now, Juliet, let's see what you've got."

"Dad, I have to tell you, first of all, that this whole thing is Joe's idea. I couldn't have done it without him."

"Well, now, that's nice of you to say."

"It's just the truth. You know how Joe likes to make things, and I'm not good at it. So he got the idea, and I did it all, but he had to show me step by step."

"Well, that's all that's necessary—that you do it yourself. Now, show me what you have here."

"It's a steam engine. See? And it really works."

"Well, let's have a demonstration."

Juliet and Joe had searched high and low for materials for her steam engine. The most difficult thing to find was the boiler. They finally found a copper container and glued the

91

top on it with superglue and then put small rivets in it so that it was tight. Joe showed her how to use copper tubing to run the escaping steam into a flywheel. So with his help she had constructed a steam engine that was very interesting.

"See, Dad, the first thing we do is fill the container with water." She did this, using a teakettle. Then she screwed the cap back on the container. "Now we light these candles under here. We could have used other things for heat, but candles were easy."

Mr. Jones looked at the eight stubby candles underneath the boiler and watched as Juliet lit them all.

"Hm. Isn't that the lighter I use to light my charcoal fires?"

"Yes, Dad. I just borrowed it."

"I know you're borrowing it. But next time I grill hamburgers, I'll be looking for this."

"I'll put it back. I'll be responsible. I promise. See, now—the candles are all lit."

Mr. Jones winked at Joe. "What happens next?"

"Well, we have to wait until the candles give off enough heat, and that makes steam out of the water."

Mr. Jones sat down, and they all chatted while the candles burned on.

Soon Juliet heard something. "You hear

that, Dad? That's the steam. Now it will come out of this tube and go into this thing here."

"And what's in there?"

"Joe calls it a turbine. He showed me how to make it. It turns. And this part, outside here, is the flywheel. Just watch now, Dad."

Soon the hissing of the steam became louder, and then Juliet cried, "See! The flywheel's turning!"

Soon the little wheel was turning faster and faster until finally it was moving too fast to be seen.

"Well, that's my project. If it were big enough, Joe says, you could hook it up and run machinery with it."

"They even ran tractors on steam engines back in the early days," Joe said.

"Well, Juliet, I must say it's going to be a tie between you and Joe as to who has made the best science project."

"Oh, Joe would have to get the credit for this! He thought of it."

"I think both of you deserve a lot of credit for the steam engine."

"You really like them, Dad? You like our projects?"

"Sure do, and to show you how much I like what you've done, I'm going to take you both out on the job with me this afternoon."

"Out where you're building the bridge?" Joe cried. "Oh boy!"

Mr. Jones, from time to time, would take them both out to where he worked. Juliet knew that some of his workplaces were a little dangerous for them to visit or were too far away. But she and Joe were always excited when they could go.

He said, "Let's go ask your mom to pack a snack for us. You help her, Juliet. And, Joe, you can help me get my tools put in the Bronco."

The two hurried off at once, both eager to get going.

Juliet helped her mother make sandwiches. "These'll be great, Mom."

"You'll need something to drink, too. I could make—"

"Oh, we can take along some Pepsis," Joe said. "Come on, Mom—we want all the time we can with Dad on the job."

"All right." Mrs. Jones laughed. She looked at her husband and said, "Be careful. And you make them be careful."

"Now, when was I not careful?"

"That's right. You always are. Well, get along with you, now."

An hour later they came to their dad's half-built bridge. Both Juliet and Joe were given yellow hard hats then, and that always made Juliet feel important. They followed their father out on one of the piers, and they were

94

very pleased to see how everyone looked to him for advice.

"It'd be nice to be an engineer," Joe whispered. "Everybody has to do what you say."

"But first you have to know *what* to say. That means going to school and studying a lot."

"I don't mind studying if I see some sense in it," Joe said.

The afternoon passed quickly. They ate their snack and watched the workers, and Joe was underfoot everywhere his father went. Juliet found it more fun to talk to some of the workmen. They were friendly and told her their names and what they were doing.

Finally, when quitting time came, they bundled into the Bronco and went home.

"Well," Mr. Jones said as they entered the house, "I liked *your* projects. How did you like my bridge?"

"It's a beautiful bridge, Dad," Juliet told him. "Can I go with you again sometime?"

"I expect you both can. Well, let's get washed up for supper." He turned to his wife and gave her a hug and said, "I'm all dirty, but I like a little affection anyway."

"You can have that some other time. Now, everybody go get ready to eat."

"Suits me," Joe said. "I'm so starved I could eat a skunk!"

"We don't have skunk," his mother said. "It's something even better."

It turned out that she had prepared a fine supper—fried chicken and gravy, mashed potatoes, green beans, and cornbread. For dessert there was pecan pie, which was Mr. Jones's favorite.

Leaning back in his chair, he said, "Well, now, I couldn't have gotten a better meal than that at McDonalds."

They all laughed at him, for everybody knew he did not like McDonalds very much. He always said he had taken them so often when they were small that he'd gotten burned out on McDonalds.

The family joined in washing dishes, singing together and making a game out of it. Afterwards they went into the family room and watched a Walt Disney video that Mrs. Jones had rented for them.

When that was over, Joe said, "This has been a fun day."

"It sure has," Juliet said. "It doesn't get much better than this. Let's go outside for a while now and take the telescope."

"I'll set it up for you," their dad said.

He had built them a telescope, grinding the lenses himself, and Juliet and Joe liked nothing much better than to go out and look at the stars—and especially at the moon—on a clear night.

For a long time they stayed in the backyard looking at the sky. Then Mr. Jones folded up the telescope to take it inside. He said, "You kids hurry on in now."

"All right, Dad. We'll be right in," Joe said. "I want to check on my bike."

As Mr. Jones went into the house, Joe crossed the yard to where they had chained their bikes against the garage. All of a sudden Juliet heard him yell. "Hey!"

"What is it?"

Joe turned to face her. In the light from the porch, his face looked white.

"What is it?" she cried again.

"My bike! Somebody stole my bike!"

"It can't be! You locked it, didn't you?"

"Yes, I locked it!" Joe said. Then he looked again. "Yours is gone, too!"

"Mine?" Juliet ran over to him. She picked up the chain and said, "The chain's been cut!"

"Mine too! Somebody had a hacksaw or bolt cutters!"

He ran toward the house then, calling out, "Dad—Dad!"

The two burst into the kitchen, and Mr. Jones met them. "What in the world is wrong?"

"Somebody stole our bikes! Both of them!" Joe cried. "Come and see."

For a time there was nothing but confusion. Mrs. Jones tried her best to calm Juliet and Joe down.

When they went back into the house, Mr. Jones said, "I'm going to call the neighbors who were on the neighborhood watch. And I'm going to call the police too."

Their father made several phone calls. Then he turned to Juliet and Joe, saying, "Nobody seems to have seen anything. Well, it's too late to do anything tonight. We'll see what we can do in the morning."

"I can't sleep tonight! There's no point in going to bed!" Joe complained.

"You go on up to bed now. Both of you. And don't worry about this until morning."

"But our beautiful bikes! They're both gone!" Juliet wailed.

"I know. It's tough. It's happened to your friends, and you were sorry for them. But now it's happened to you, and that's different, isn't it?"

Juliet realized that it *was* different. She had been truly sorry for Chili, and for Sam, and for Billy, and for Jack, and for Jenny, but now it was her own bike that was gone. She said slowly, "I didn't really know what it was like when I was just hearing about it."

"Yeah," Joe said. "It gives you a funny feeling inside."

"As I say, don't worry about it. They're bicycles. They're *only* bicycles. They can be replaced."

"But they were *our* bicycles!" Juliet said. "They were special to us!"

Mr. Jones put an arm around each of them. "It's a hard lesson, but life is like that sometimes. We lose things as we go along. But remember, God has something good for you out of this. There's a verse in the Bible that says something like, 'I will restore to you the years that the locusts have eaten.' I think God was talking about when we lose something important to us. It may take a while, but if we obey and trust Him, the Lord will either give it back to us or—more often—something a lot better."

"Well, if God said it, then it's so," Juliet said.

"Now, you two go ahead upstairs. Say your prayers and just tell the Lord Jesus about it. It'll be all right."

Juliet followed Joe up the stairs. She got ready for bed and had her prayer time. Then she lay awake for a long time, trying to think of what to do. Finally she prayed, "Lord, I'm sorry to lose the bike. It makes me think about what kind of people would take it. So I guess I'll just pray for them too. They have to be very unhappy people to go around stealing things. So help them, whoever they are. You know them, and I don't."

Next, she began thinking about what it must be like to live the kind of life where you stole things for a living. It made her feel very sad.

Finally she settled down to go to sleep with Boots purring on her pillow. She stroked him and said, "I'm glad they stole a bike instead of you. I can get another bike, but I could never get another Boots."

10

The Stakeout

This has been the worst day I've ever had,"
Juliet said. She looked across the school-
room at Joe, who was sitting at his desk with
his chin propped on his palm. "I can't think
of anything but our bicycles."

"Me either," he said glumly. He suddenly
leaned over and beat his head on the desk,
making a thumping noise. "I feel so stupid!
So stupid!"

"Don't talk like that, Joe."

"Well, don't you feel stupid?"

Juliet asked, "What did you do that was
stupid?"

"I don't know. But if I had been smart, they
wouldn't have got my bicycle."

"I don't know what you could have done.
You had it chained. You can't stay up and
watch it every night."

"They must have come in when we were eating supper. Just clipped the chains and made off with the bikes."

"We couldn't see any clues last night. It was too dark. But I bet we could find something this morning."

They both had begged to be let off from schoolwork, but Mrs. Jones had been firm. "No," she'd said, "you do your work first, and this afternoon you can go outside."

Juliet got up and walked to the window. She looked out and saw Boots climbing a tree, trying to catch a cardinal. He never caught one, but he never seemed to give up. "It looks like that cat would learn sooner or later that he can't catch a bird."

Joe did not answer. He was looking straight at the wall, apparently not seeing it. "We don't even have any way to go anywhere."

"What do you mean? We can walk."

"Walk?"

"Yes, walk!"

"I don't want to walk. I've had a bicycle since I was six years old. I've ridden one everywhere I've ever gone."

Juliet returned to her desk. "Well, now you're going to have to learn to walk. Dad said he'd replace our bicycles if we don't find the old ones. He just doesn't have the money right now."

"I know. I'm not really complaining, but it's just going to be different."

Their mother came into the classroom and saw the two of them just sitting there. "Have you got all your work done?"

"Not quite," Joe said quickly. He made an attempt to look busy, then looked at his mother and said, "Aw, Mom, let us go out. I can't get my mind on studying."

"I can't either," Juliet said.

Mrs. Jones looked surprised—not at Joe but at Juliet. "Why, Juliet, you never have trouble studying!"

"I'm having trouble now. Please, Mom. Let us go outside and see what we can find. We can study this afternoon. We'll make it up."

Their mother hesitated, and Joe said, "Please, Mom."

"Oh, I guess it'll be all right this one time— but you'll have to make it up this afternoon."

"Yeah, we'll do that, Mom. Sure we will," Joe said. He jumped up, and Juliet followed him as he raced down the stairs.

They went at once to the garage and for some time went over the ground carefully, looking for clues. They did find some faint footprints, but the ground was so hard they couldn't tell what they were. Juliet was disappointed.

But when they went out by the street, she found a Fudgy wrapper in the gutter.

"A Fudgy wrapper!" she cried.

"It's just like they're leaving a trail. Whoever that guy is, he must eat Fudgys all the time."

"Well, we're pretty sure the thief is the candy eater," Juliet said. "But I wish we had gotten some footprints. We could have checked them against the casts we made."

Joe squinted, thinking. "You know, down at the end of our street there's that new construction. There's nothing but dirt and mud there. If they rode the bicycles that way, I'll bet we could find some prints."

"Joe, you're getting to be 'Too Smart.'"

"Let's go have a look."

Juliet and Joe ran down the street to the site of the new house and began looking for tracks. They did not find anything right away, but suddenly Joe yelled, "Look here, Juliet!"

She ran to him and looked down to where he was pointing. "There they are," he said. "Two sets of bicycle tracks."

"But they could be anybody's bicycles," Juliet said. "I wouldn't know the tread on ours. Would you?"

"Sure I would. My bike makes this tread here. See, it looks like big X's. I don't know what yours looks like, but this is my bike for sure."

"Then the other one is mine. Now we're getting somewhere. Let's follow them."

It was easy to follow the tracks in the soft

dirt. But when they got away from the new construction area, whoever had been riding the bicycles moved over onto the soft grass.

"Good thing it rained last night. You can still see the wheel tracks. They're headed right toward downtown." Juliet's heart began to beat faster.

"What will we do if we see the thieves?" Joe asked. "Will we just run up and grab them?"

"Of course not. They'll be too big for that. They're probably grown-ups. We'd better go get Chief Bender."

"I guess so," Joe said. "Looks like maybe the tracks are turning here. You go that way and see. I'll go ahead and around the block. I'll meet you at the other end."

"All right, Joe. Just be careful."

Juliet was a little nervous by now. She followed what looked like faint tracks as far as the street behind the buildings, and then she lost all sign of them. She kept walking, though, studying the sidewalk at her feet, until she came to a narrow alley. And then Too Smart Jones knew where she was.

She peered down the alley. She could see nobody, but as Juliet hesitated, she thought she heard something. *It's voices again. And they're coming from down this alley.*

For a while she stood listening, and then she saw Joe coming around the block from the other way. She motioned to him.

As he came running, she put a finger on her lips and signaled for him to be silent. He came up, and she whispered, "Did you find any tracks?"

"No, I couldn't find anything. Did you? And why are you being so quiet?"

"Because I hear somebody down this alley again."

Joe turned his head to one side. "I hear loud talking, that's all."

"What if it's them?"

"The bicycle thieves?" Joe looked startled. "You think it could be them?"

"It could be. The tracks led to this street, and we can't follow them any farther."

"Let's go into the alley," Joe said.

Juliet hesitated. "I don't think Mom and Dad would like it if we did that."

"I suppose not. Well, let's just wait here for a while then. Maybe they'll come out."

"Yes, let's. We'll watch and see who comes. That's what the police call a stakeout."

The idea had sounded good, but time passed very slowly. After maybe a half hour went by and nothing happened, Joe said, "I'm thirsty."

"Why don't you go get us some sodas while we watch?"

"Sounds good to me. I'll go over to Mr. Simpson's. What do you want?"

"Get me a root beer."

"All right. If you see anybody, just keep out of sight behind the Dumpster."

"I will."

Joe left, and Juliet stood watch. She stayed behind the Dumpster but was able to peer out and keep an eye on the alley.

"There's probably nobody there now," she said to herself. She was getting tired and wished that she had just left with Joe.

But then she heard a sound, and she peeked out quickly. Movement was taking place in the alley! Juliet ducked out of sight. And then she heard the rattling of bicycle spokes. She peeked out again from behind the Dumpster, and her heart leaped. Two boys with long hair were coming up the alley. Both were riding new bikes, and they were coming right toward her.

Juliet ducked as far behind the Dumpster as she could go, her heart beating rapidly. *What if they catch me?* she thought.

She heard the bicycles getting closer and closer. Now she could hear the two boys talking to each other. Finally she could make out, by the sounds, that they had turned out onto the street.

Cautiously she poked her head out. There they went, down the street. She was sorry she had not seen their faces. *I don't recognize the bicycles either,* she thought. *But they weren't mine or Joe's. I could see that much.*

She started to run after them, then realized that the boys on the bicycles were too fast for her. At the end of the street she ran into Joe returning. "Did you see them? Did you see them?"

He had two soda pops, one in each hand. "Did I see who?"

"Those two boys on bicycles!"

"No, I didn't see anybody. You mean you let them get away?"

Juliet said sharply, "What was I supposed to do?"

Joe handed her the root beer. "I should have stayed here."

Juliet felt insulted. "You couldn't have done anything I didn't do!"

"Did you get a good look at them? I could've gotten a look at them. We should have had a camera with us. That would have been evidence."

Juliet wished she had thought of that. "We'll start carrying a camera from now on."

"You don't even have a camera. We'll get one of that throwaway kind." Joe sighed. "OK, then. Did you see the bikes they were on?"

"I got a glimpse of them but mostly from the back. It was hard to tell anything. But they weren't our bikes. I know that. They looked new. One was white, and the other one was dark green."

"I sure wish I'd been here," Joe muttered. "Maybe if we'd run fast enough, we could have caught them."

"No, we couldn't have. I tried. Let's go back down to the alley where they came from and see if we can find anything."

Juliet and Joe cautiously started down the alley. It was just an alley like any other, and they found nothing in it. Almost nothing.

Halfway into the alley, Juliet looked down and said, "Uh-oh!"

"What is it?" Joe came up beside her.

Juliet leaned over. "A Fudgy wrapper!"

Joe seemed to hold his breath. "I think we've got something now."

"And I think you're right. It's time to go to the police," Juliet said. "Maybe they won't listen to us because we're just kids."

"Chief Bender will listen."

"Yeah. I guess he would. He's always liked us. Let's go, then."

Juliet and Joe left the alley and ran toward the police station. As they went, Joe said, "We've got to get a skateboard or something. This walking is killing me."

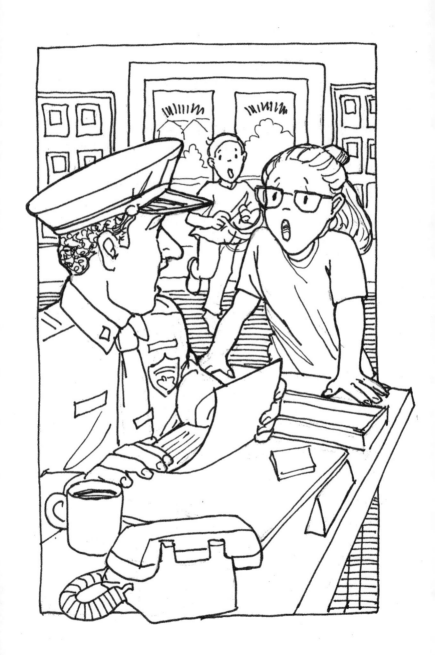

11

Chief Bender

The police chief of Oakwood was a big man with black hair and dark brown eyes. He was sitting behind his desk when Juliet and Joe rushed in. "And what are you two doing here all out of breath?" he asked.

Juliet was gasping and had to pause for a moment. She and Joe had run all the way from the alley to the police station. Finally she was able to say, "Chief, you've got to do something! We've found some suspects!"

"Suspects for what?"

"The people who have been stealing the bicycles. We found them."

"Oh?" Instantly Chief Bender grew interested. "Where are they?"

"Well," Juliet said, "we don't have them with us. But I saw two of them."

"How do you know? Where were they? What were they doing?"

"Joe and I followed their trail from our house. Oh, I forgot to tell you! Our bikes were stolen, too."

"I know. Your father called me."

"Anyway, we found the tracks of the bicycles. And look—we found this."

Juliet reached into her pocket and drew out the plastic envelope that her mother used for freezing vegetables. She kept her evidence in that. She handed it to the chief, who opened the plastic bag and looked at the candy paper.

"This is just a candy wrapper."

"It's a Fudgy wrapper, and we've found them before." Juliet went on to explain that they had found Fudgy wrappers where other bicycles had been stolen. "It has to be them, doesn't it?"

"Not necessarily, Juliet. Maybe lots of people eat Fudgy bars."

"Did you ever taste one?" Joe asked.

"No. I don't eat candy."

"They taste awful! Mr. Simpson has them in his store, but he says he doesn't sell many."

"Well, that's something of interest. But not enough to arrest anybody on."

"That's not all," Juliet told him. "I was standing down at that alley off of Cedar Street, and I heard voices, so Joe and I staked out the place."

Chief Bender raised his eyebrows. "You're

112

getting real scientific. Or have you been watching those crime shows on TV again?"

"Well, that's what they call it. Anyway, I was watching, and I saw them."

"Did you see them, too, Joe?"

"No, I'd gone off to get some soda pop."

"Left your sister all alone?"

"Well, she said she was thirsty."

"And what did you see, Juliet?"

"We stayed there a long time, and nothing happened. And then after Joe left, I heard these voices. So I hid behind the Dumpster. And then I heard them coming."

"Heard who coming?"

"I didn't know who it was, but they were riding bicycles. I was afraid they'd see me, so I got behind the Dumpster."

"Did you get a good look at them?"

Juliet hesitated. "No, I didn't. I was afraid they'd see me, like I said. So by the time I looked out, they were halfway down the block and riding pretty fast. All I could see was that they had long hair, they were maybe high school boys, and they wore blue jeans."

"Not too helpful a description."

"It was all I could see."

"I told her if I'd been there, I would have taken a picture. If I'd had a camera."

Chief Bender grinned. "You're like the fellow that said, 'I'll have some ham and eggs if you have some eggs.'"

"Joe couldn't have done any better than I did!" Juliet protested. "But I *am* going to carry a camera with me from now on and take pictures of everything that even looks suspicious."

Chief Bender sat back in his chair and took a deep breath. "Look, Juliet, do you know how many high school boys we have in this town?"

"Well, I don't know. Several hundred, I suppose."

"That's right. At least. You know how many of them have bicycles?"

Juliet looked down at her feet. "A lot, I guess."

"Several hundred," Chief Bender said. "So the two boys you saw could have been anybody. And one candy wrapper doesn't mean you have a case."

"You mean you can't do anything?"

"We're doing all we can, Juliet," Chief Bender said.

"I guess we just got too excited," Joe said. "Come on, Juliet."

Juliet protested, but Joe dragged her outside. "He can't do anything with just one candy wrapper. Let's get out of here."

After finishing their schoolwork that afternoon, Juliet and Joe went over to the Del Rio house, where they found Sam and Delores practicing their gymnastics. First, they told the Del Rios about their bicycle adventure, and then they sat and watched as their friends did backflips. It was amazing the way they could simply leap into the air, tuck their bodies into a ball, roll over, and land on their feet.

"I'd give anything if I could do that," Joe said.

Sam turned to look at him. He was wearing a pair of shorts and a white T-shirt today. "No, you wouldn't."

"What do you mean I wouldn't?"

"I mean it takes hard work and lots of practice. Besides, you have to start when you're very young."

Juliet laughed. "You're very young *now!*"

"We started when we were three or four. I can't even remember when." Delores smiled. "Our parents taught us."

"Teach me how to do a backflip."

"Well, you have to start out on the trampoline. Come around back, and I'll show you."

The four of them trailed around to the backyard, where the trampoline was set up.

Juliet said, "I've always been afraid of these things. I'm afraid I'll hit my head on the edge."

"I've heard about people doing that," Joe cut in. "You can get paralyzed on a trampoline."

"But this is a big one. If you stay right in the middle, you can't get hurt. I'll show you."

Juliet and Joe took an hour of backflip lessons from the Del Rio children. They were not very good at it, but it was fun.

Delores said, "If you'd practice every day for a month, you'll be ready to try something harder."

"I don't have time for that," Juliet said.

"Neither do I," Joe said.

"You see! I told you!" Sam said triumphantly. "You don't really want to turn a backflip. I mean you don't want to learn how. You just want to do it."

Juliet nodded. "I guess that's right. I know some kids who think they want to play the piano, but they don't want to practice. I thought I did, but I didn't know that meant I was going to be taking lessons, practicing for hours, and all of that."

"But you play so well now," Delores said. "It's worth it, isn't it?"

"Yes, it's worth it now, but a lot of people don't want to put in the time."

"That's the way it is with gymnastics," Sam said. "It takes lots of practice."

Mr. Del Rio came out then and watched them for a while. He said thoughtfully, "I think a lot about my days with the circus."

"Was it fun, Mr. Del Rio?"

"Fun but a lot of work. We had to move everything in big trucks. When we left town, we had to pack up everything, and that was nothing but hard work."

"But didn't you have people to do that?"

"All of us had to help. You had to be tough

in those days. You worked for hours for that little five minutes you got under the lights. But it was worth it," he said. "I still remember the applause and the people shouting."

"I hope I can do that when I get older," Delores said.

"The circus is about gone these days," her grandfather said. "Except in Europe. What are you kids up to besides practicing acrobatics?"

"We've been trying to do something to find the people who are stealing bicycles."

"Better leave that to the police," Mr. Del Rio advised.

After their grandfather left, Delores said, "You want to go upstairs and play dress up?"

"I just don't feel like it today."

Joe said, "*I* think we ought to go back to that alley."

Juliet looked at him. He usually did not get into her mystery investigations. She said, "You really want to do that?"

"Well, I lost my bicycle, didn't I? I'm going to take any chance I can to get it back."

"Wouldn't you be afraid if you saw the thieves?" Delores asked.

"I wouldn't feel too good about it," Joe admitted. "But if we actually saw somebody riding a bicycle that we knew—like yours, Sam, or like mine—then we'd have something to take to the police."

Juliet made up her mind. "Then let's go back."

It took some doing to get permission from Mr. and Mrs. Del Rio. Even then, they did not tell Sam and Delores's grandparents they were going to look for bicycle thieves.

"We want to go down and get some ice cream and go by the park," Sam told them.

"All right, but you be home early."

"That wasn't exactly the truth, Sam," Delores said as they left the house.

"But we *are* going to get some ice cream, and we *do* go by the park. If we stop off at the alley on the way, that's something else."

Somehow that bothered Juliet.

It also seemed to bother Delores. She said, "Sometimes I think telling a half-truth is worse than telling a whole lie!"

"I didn't lie!" Sam said. "I said we were going to get ice cream and go by the park, and we are."

"Now, Sam," Delores argued, "you know we're really going to go to that alley and look for those thieves."

The argument went on, and Juliet got on Delores's side. "I think Delores is right," she said. "It's real tempting to get what we want by not telling the whole truth."

So far, Joe had said little, but now even he said, "Uh . . . Sam . . . I hate to say it, but I'm siding with the girls."

Sam did not say anything for a while, as they continued to trudge on. Then he said, "I guess you're right. You want to go home, Delores?"

"Not now," she said. "But maybe we ought to tell them about it when we get home. And next time we'll tell them the whole truth to start with."

"Yeah, let's do that," Sam said.

They reached town and stopped in to get ice cream. Juliet tried lime, which she did not like very much.

Then they left the shop and headed toward the alley. When they got there, Juliet said, "Listen to that. I can hear loud talking again."

"I hear it, too," Delores said. "They sure are noisy. Did you go into the alley last time?"

"Not while they were there," Juliet said.

"And we're not going to do that," Joe said firmly. "I know our parents wouldn't like it. But we can watch from out here in the street."

They stationed themselves across the street for what seemed a long time, and nothing happened. Juliet decided this was going to take a lot of patience.

But then suddenly Delores cried, "Somebody's coming up the alley!"

The group scattered so they wouldn't look like a group, as Juliet had instructed them.

Juliet watched two older men come out of the alley. As they passed by on the other side of the street, she heard them discussing a car they had been working on. One man turned his head and looked straight at Juliet, and her heart jumped into her throat. But then he simply walked on.

"Yikes, I thought he was going to come and get us," Joe said from behind her.

Juliet jumped. "Don't scare me like that!"

"Scare you? I just spoke to you. That's not against the law, is it?"

Sam and Delores joined them. "I don't think those two were bicycle thieves. They just look like workmen," Sam said.

At that moment, Juliet heard someone calling her name. "Hey, Too Smart, what's going on?"

She looked up the street to see Flash Gordon wheeling himself in their direction.

He turned around in a spin in front of them as he often did. "What's happening?" he asked.

Juliet said, "We think that the bicycle thieves are down here in this alley."

"What makes you think that?" He listened as Juliet told him the story, and then he said, "Why don't you go to the police?"

"We have been to the police," Joe said. "But Chief Bender said we didn't have any evidence."

"If you think this is where they're hiding out, we can take turns watching."

"I don't know, Flash. Maybe we ought to go on home," Juliet said. She was feeling more and more that they were doing the wrong thing. "After all," she said, "this is police business. That's what my dad says."

But Flash was getting excited. He said, "But we're here, and we really need to find out who's stealing these bikes!"

At that moment there was a noise in the alley, and a boy on a bicycle pedaled out. Juliet saw that it was the boy that they had seen before.

And then Joe shouted, "Hey, you, that's *my* bike!"

The boy put on the brakes and yelled something.

Almost instantly, Juliet saw more boys spill into the alley and start toward them. "Let's get out of here!" she cried, and the group broke and fled.

Juliet ran for all she was worth. When she had gotten half a block away, she looked around and saw that everyone was with her—everyone except Flash.

"Where's Flash?" she asked, stopping.

"I think they got him," Joe panted.

"They did," Sam gasped. "I saw them grab his wheelchair and pull him back into that alley."

"This time Chief Bender's got to help!" Juliet cried.

121

They ran as hard as they could toward the police station. Fortunately, before they got there, they ran into Chief Bender leaning against his patrol car and talking into the radio.

Juliet screamed, "Chief, come on! We found the thieves in that alley, and they've got Flash!"

"Flash Gordon? The boy in the wheelchair?"

"Yes! And this time we've got evidence. We saw this guy riding Joe's bike. We can identify it."

"All right. Let me call for backup." Chief Bender spoke into the mike that was in his hand. "Investigation at Cedar and Sixth. Officer requests assistance." Then he said, "Get in the car."

The four piled into the backseat of the squad car, and Chief Bender took off at once for the alley. He stopped before they got there and said, "We'll have to wait here. You say there's several of them?"

"Maybe four or five. I don't know how many," Juliet said.

"Now, they may be armed. I want you kids out of this. You understand that? You stay right here in the car."

"I understand, Chief," Juliet said. "We all do." Her heart was pounding. She turned to Joe, saying, "What's happening to Flash? I'm worried."

"Me too."

The four youngsters sat in the squad car, waiting and quiet. Juliet was tense.

Chief Bender said nothing, but his face was set in a frown. Then he looked back and said, "Here comes the other car. You kids stay right here. You understand? No fooling, Juliet!"

"Yes sir. We understand."

Chief Bender got out, and they watched as three officers jumped out of the other squad car. Chief Bender motioned to them, and they all disappeared down the alley.

"I just hope Flash is all right," Juliet said, and she began asking the Lord to help him.

12

The Rescue

Flash Gordon was sitting in his wheelchair. He looked down at his arms, which were being tied to the chair's armrests. Then he looked up at the two boys who were tying him. He said, "You don't really have to tie me like that. I'm not going anywhere."

"We're making sure of that!" The speaker was the same boy that Flash had seen earlier. He had stringy hair tied in a ponytail. Now he looked closely at Flash. "I've seen you before."

"Yes. I saw you a few days ago."

"You were with a bunch of other kids, weren't you?"

"That's right. My name's Flash Gordon."

The boy laughed. "My name's John Smith."

Flash knew that was not his real name. He looked around at the large storage room they were in, and he saw at least fifteen bicycles.

One of them he recognized instantly as belonging to Samuel Del Rio. His hands were tied firmly now. "What are you going to do with me?" he asked.

One of the other fellows, a pudgy boy of about sixteen with a fat face and little piggish eyes, said, "Getting worried, are you?"

"No, I'm not worried. I'm just curious."

The pudgy boy said, "You can't kid me! You're worried. You'd have to be."

"No, I'm not really worried," Flash said easily. "God knows where I am."

A third boy paced around nervously. He was taller and was probably closer to eighteen. He seemed very jumpy. "We've got to do something," he said. "Those kids are going to bring somebody back."

"We're going to do something. We're going to get out of here," the one who called himself John Smith said. He looked around with regret. "We went to all the work of snatching these bikes, and now we have to leave them."

The pudgy-faced fellow said, "This one will yell for help as soon as we go."

"No, he won't." John Smith whipped out a handkerchief and said, "I'm going to have to gag you, fella."

"I wish you wouldn't do that," Flash said, eyeing the dirty handkerchief. "I give you my word I won't call for help."

John Smith laughed gruffly. "Why should I believe you?"

"Because I always tell the truth."

"Sure! I got your word for it, don't I?"

"I'm a Christian, and I always try to tell the truth."

"A Bible thumper, huh! Well," the pasty-faced one said, "I don't believe any of that stuff."

"It's true, though. I've been a Christian since I was eight years old."

"So why can't you walk? Why don't you just ask God to heal you?" John Smith demanded with a laugh.

"God is going to heal me."

"When?"

"When He gets ready. God always does what's best for us. Right now He thinks it's best for me to be in this wheelchair. But one day I'll get out of it and walk—if that's what He wants."

The three boys listened with disbelief on their faces.

And then Flash smiled. "I know the one thing you guys need."

"We need money and fast cars! That's what we need!"

"No, you need Jesus. You need to be saved."

"What are you talking about?" the pasty-faced one asked. "Saved from what?"

"Saved from being lost. Jesus died to save all of us." Flash began talking rapidly, for he knew he could not hold their attention long. As quickly as he could, he told them that everyone was lost because everyone has sinned, but Jesus died in their place to take away their sin.

The boy called John Smith said, "We haven't got time for this!" He quickly put the handkerchief over Flash's mouth, tied it firmly, and said, "Now, let's get out of here!"

The three boys headed for the door, and the taller one opened it. But just as he did, a big man came crashing in, followed by three others in police uniforms.

"You guys stand fast!" Chief Bender said. His gun was drawn, and he looked around quickly. "You've hurt that boy, and you'll be in real trouble! And not just for stealing bicycles."

"He's all right," John Smith said quickly, his hands in the air.

"Put the cuffs on them," Chief Bender said. While the officers were doing that, he came over to Flash and removed the gag.

"Are you all right, Flash?"

"I'm fine. They didn't hurt me. You might untie my hands, though."

The chief undid the ropes holding his arms, and Flash rubbed his wrists. "Kind of cut the circulation off," he said.

"Well, I'm glad you're all right. You had me

worried when Juliet came roaring in to tell me you'd been captured."

"Can I have a word with these fellas?"

"These guys? Why, I guess so."

"Hey, guys, I know you'll be in jail tonight. I'll be down to see you later. I'll bring you some Bibles."

"You can keep your Bibles," the tallest of the three said.

"No, you need a Bible," Flash said. "And I'll bring my dad with me, too. You all need to be saved. He'll tell you how better than I could."

"Take 'em down and lock 'em up," Chief Bender said. "Come on, Flash. Your friends are worried about you."

"Oh, that's right!" Flash wheeled his way out of the warehouse, and as soon as he was in the street, the chief's car suddenly began to unload. Juliet was the first to get to him, concern on her face.

"Are you all right, Flash?"

"Oh, sure. I'm fine. They didn't hurt me a bit."

"Whew, I'm glad to hear that," Joe said. "We were worried."

"As a matter of fact, I got a chance to preach at 'em a little bit. Not much, but I told them how God's going to heal me if He wants to and how He wants to save them."

Sam Del Rio looked at Flash in wonderment. "I can't believe you preached at those guys after the way they treated you."

"They didn't treat me so bad. And now I've got something to do."

"What's that?" Delores asked.

"I told them I'd go to the jail tonight and bring 'em some Bibles."

"You think they'll read them?" Sam asked, his eyebrows going up.

"I don't know whether they will or not, but I'm going to bring the Bibles and bring my dad. I feel sorry for guys like that."

"I do, too," Juliet said. "And did you notice the tall one? He had on cowboy boots. I'll bet they'll match the cast we made."

Chief Bender came up in time to hear this. "Cast of what?" He listened as Juliet explained what they had done. Then he said, "That'll be another bit of evidence. We won't need much. I think they were getting ready to move the bicycles out in a truck, but they won't be doing that now. You want to come along and see if you can identify some of them?"

Eagerly Juliet and her friends went down the alley and into the warehouse. She found her own bicycle almost at once. She put her hands on it and beamed at the chief. "This is mine!"

"And this is mine!" Joe said.

Soon Sam had claimed his.

"I expect we'll find all the owners. Most of

them have filed reports," Chief Bender said. "Well, you'd better get home and tell your folks about all of this."

They wheeled their bikes outside. Delores got on behind Sam, and he started pedaling toward the Del Rio house. Juliet and Joe started for home.

Joe did not try to get ahead of her for once. He let her stay even with him. He seemed to be thinking hard.

Juliet glanced at him. "What are you thinking about?"

"I was just feeling sorry for those guys. They're not much older than we are. The fat-faced one couldn't be over fourteen."

"They aren't very old."

"What's going to happen to them?"

"Well," Juliet said sadly, "I guess, if they're found guilty, they'll be locked up someplace."

"In a prison?"

"No, I think they send young ones like that to boot camp—or reform school, maybe."

Joe did not say anything for a time. Then he said, "I wish they hadn't gotten into stealing. I still can't help feeling sorry for them."

When they reached home, Juliet and Joe went in to tell their mother what had happened.

Mrs. Jones listened carefully, then said very seriously, "And how many times have your father and I told you to let the police do police things?"

Both Juliet and Joe hung their heads and said they had been wrong.

"It won't happen again, Mom," Juliet promised.

"Well, I'm glad that mystery is over, anyway. Now we won't have to worry about bicycles."

"You know what Flash is going to do, Mom? He's going to go to the jail tonight with his dad—to talk to those boys."

"I think that's fine. They need somebody to help them, and Flash's father is very good at that. He holds services at the jail all the time."

"Do you suppose I could go with them, Mom?" Juliet asked.

Joe nodded. "And me too?"

"You'll have to talk to Mr. Gordon about that. Why don't you call and ask?"

When Juliet called, Flash's dad answered the phone. "Flash just got home," he said, "and he told me what happened."

"He thought you would want to go and talk to those boys—and maybe give them Bibles?"

"We're going tonight."

"Do you think Joe and I could go with you?"

"Sure. It would be a good experience for you. And it might do those young fellows some good to see the folks they had wronged still love them. I'll be by to pick you up at seven o'clock."

Juliet hung up the phone and nodded to her mother and Joe. "He said it's all right."

"Good," Joe said. "Now let's go out and just sit on our bikes."

They went to the garage and ran their hands lovingly over the bicycles.

"It's a miracle we got these back," he said. "Another day and they probably would have been gone forever."

Juliet nodded. "I believe you. I'm never going to take my bicycle for granted again."

"*Mrow!*"

Juliet looked down to see Boots at her feet. He began pushing his head against her leg. She picked up the cat, saying, "Boots wants to go for a bike ride."

"Then let's go. I'll race you."

"You always win, Joe."

"No, this time I'll let you win."

They got on the bikes and started down the street. Juliet held Boots against her shoulder. From time to time he would say, "*Mrow!*" and she would say, "Be careful, Boots. I wouldn't want anything to happen to you."

Too Smart Jones thought about the case of the missing bicycles. She thought about the boys sitting in jail. "I'll have to tell them how wonderful the Lord's been to me," she whispered to Boots.

And Boots once again said, "*Mrow!*"

Get swept away in the many Gilbert Morris Adventures available from Moody Press:

"Too Smart" Jones

4025-8 Pool Party Thief
4026-6 Buried Jewels
4027-4 Disappearing Dogs
4028-2 Dangerous Woman
4029-0 Stranger in the Cave
4030-4 Cat's Secret
4031-2 Stolen Bicycles
4032-0 Wilderness Mystery
4033-9 Spooky Mansion
4034-7 Mysterious Artist

Come along for the adventures and mysteries Juliet "Too Smart" Jones always manages to find. She and her other homeschool friends solve these great adventures and learn biblical truths along the way. Ages 9-14

Seven Sleepers - The Lost Chronicles

3667-6 The Spell of the Crystal Chair
3668-4 The Savage Game of Lord Zarak
3669-2 The Strange Creatures of Dr. Korbo
3670-6 City of the Cyborgs
3671-4 The Temptations of Pleasure Island
3672-2 Victims of Nimbo
3673-0 The Terrible Beast of Zor

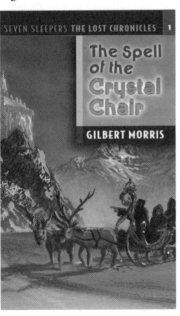

More exciting adventures from the Seven Sleepers. As these exciting young people attempt to faithfully follow Goél, they learn important moral and spiritual lessons. Come along with them as they encounter danger, intrigue, and mystery. Ages 10-14

Dixie Morris Animal Adventures

Follow the exciting adventures of this animal lover as she learns more of God and His character through her many adventures underneath the Big Top.
Ages 9-14

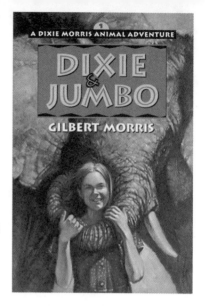

The Daystar Voyages

Join the crew of the Daystar as they traverse the wide expanse of space. Adventure and danger abound, but they learn time and again that God is truly the Master of the Universe.
Ages 10-14

MOODY
The Name You Can Trust
1-800-678-8812   www.MoodyPress.org

Seven Sleepers Series

3681-1 Flight of the Eagles
3682-X The Gates of Neptune
3683-3 The Swords of Camelot
3684-6 The Caves That Time Forgot
3685-4 Winged Riders of the Desert
3686-2 Empress of the Underworld
3687-0 Voyage of the Dolphin
3691-9 Attack of the Amazons
3692-7 Escape with the Dream Maker
3693-5 The Final Kingdom

Go with Josh and his friends as they are sent by Goél, their spiritual leader, on dangerous and challenging voyages to conquer the forces of darkness in the new world. Ages 10-14

Bonnets and Bugles Series

0911-3 Drummer Boy at Bull Run
0912-1 Yankee Belles in Dixie
0913-X The Secret of Richmond Manor
0914-8 The Soldier Boy's Discovery
0915-6 Blockade Runner
0916-4 The Gallant Boys of Gettysburg
0917-2 The Battle of Lookout Mountain
0918-0 Encounter at Cold Harbor
0919-9 Fire Over Atlanta
0920-2 Bring the Boys Home

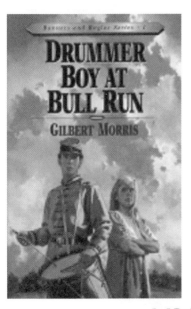

Follow good friends Leah Carter and Jeff Majors as they experience danger, intrigue, compassion, and love in these civil war adventures. Ages 10-14